TWO SPINSTERS AND A THIEF

EVE TARRINGTON

To my mother, with love.

1

Miss Judith St Clair had spent a year thinking of a way to tell her father of her secret engagement.

On the first of September, she stood near the door to his library, listening to him expound at length on the subject of Michaelmas to Mr Barnwell, his curate. Judith knew her father's thoughts on the subject by heart. "Papa," she said, but her voice was not loud enough to carry. She clutched the letter that her fiancé had written to her father. Nearly a year old, it was still sealed.

Their engagement had begun in the summer. The autumn was easy enough, as Judith had to help her friend with a personal matter. Miss Louisa-Margaretta Haddington was herself considering a proposal, and only with Judith's gentle and unwavering support was she able to keep herself from accepting a very unsuitable man. Judith had no trouble convincing herself that she ought to wait, a natural deference to her friend's difficulties.

Then came winter, when Mr St Clair caught a mysterious illness that very nearly took his life. Judith wondered if he had simply been waiting for his children to recover from the first wave of grief that had taken them after they lost their mother. For quite a time, he had been steadfast, then when his children seemed to be well, he was struck down. Judith had grieved most bitterly for Mama, but only sometime later did she realise that her siblings had all been similarly distraught. Miriam's desire for a quick marriage and a new family, her brothers' exuberance that bordered on anger, and even her aunt Leah's constant meddling all were expressions of the same dark feelings, and Judith knew that her father had felt the need to be strong. She had explained to her fiancé that unwelcome news might kill her father, and he'd seen the prudence of waiting to make the announcement.

In the spring, after much persuasion from his bishop, his patroness, and his children, the rector took on Mr Barnwell, the first curate who had assisted him. Judith saw a change in Papa almost immediately. He was happier, less hurried, and more animated in all of his duties. The only trouble was ensuring that he did not give Mr Barnwell too little work, keeping the greater share for himself. That change, Judith decided, merited another delay. Morgan, her fiancé, was eager to visit, and he made it clear that he was not pleased to be kept waiting. But he was busy establishing himself as a barrister, and long days at the Inns of Court occupied his mind. He did not shy away from telling Judith that he was pursuing such a course in order to support a wife and family, and he took a great deal of pride in his decision. Judith, who knew Morgan's interest in the law to be superficial, took it as a great compliment.

In the summer, the two of them quarrelled.

It was not easy to quarrel by means of secret letters, but Judith accomplished it. She had a friend in London whose discretion could be depended upon. And so she wrote letters to Letty with her words to Morgan included in the middle of the missive, disguised as "something I have read of late in a novel that I thought might interest you" and peppered with initials instead of names. The device was bound to wear thin, but it ensured that any individual letter would not cause a scandal if discovered.

Morgan stated that he would visit his relatives at Wycliff Castle in September, just before Michaelmas. Given the demands of the Inns of Court, it would be a short visit, but it would be the first he had seen of Judith in an entire year. The visit would give him a chance to plead his case before her father, perhaps somehow arguing that he was more of a brother in the Lord's eyes than a heretic.

Morgan was a member of the Society of Friends, and as much as Judith wished she could persuade her family that his religion was similar to theirs, she knew they would take it amiss. If her father forbade the marriage outright, she would not lose financially, as he had very little money to settle on her. But losing his blessing and the company of all her siblings was not a risk she was willing to take.

As she waited at the door, she heard Mr Barnwell joking with her father.

"We should not have to plan so much if we were Quakers! We could spend the morning of Michaelmas in silence then go and eat roast goose without having thought one whit about the Lord's word."

"You needn't speak of the Quakers, sir," said her father, his voice wavering.

Judith paused. She fingered the letter, which was quite worn. For some time, she had wondered what her father would make of the date that Morgan had written upon it.

She would have to continue to wonder, for there was no

chance of her telling him at present, not when she would have to interrupt the conversation about the horrors of the Quaker faith.

Biting her lip and holding her head low, Judith ascended the stairs and took refuge in her bedchamber. She had decided to write to Morgan by way of Letty that very evening so she might report on any progress, so there was no point in that. She ended up sitting on her bed, gazing dully at the wall, letting her eyes close for what she told herself would only be a moment.

"Judith," said Moses, "you promised that you would help me with my sums."

He was frowning, his blue eyes narrowed in anticipation of the difficult task. Judith worried that Moses might be falling behind his brothers in his studies. Though their father was patient enough, he simply could not understand why his son could not seem to write or remember numbers. Even when Moses said forty-two, he might well write two hundred and forty or perhaps only a solitary little four. Judith had, by means of covering parts of the boy's work with paper, managed to help him check the accuracy of his calculations. Still, he wrote little that did not require extensive correction, and he was well aware of being alone in that. Miriam had always found mathematics to be simple if boring, and Judith had excelled in that area of study from a young age. Their other brothers seemed to do well enough at the work, though their view on the subject was closer to Miriam's. Only Judith and Papa truly enjoyed the little ciphers.

"Of course, Moses." Judith climbed wearily off her bed. As she followed her brother, she wondered what it would be like to say farewell to him for the last time. *Will Papa consider me part of the family if I marry outside the church?* They had never had a family member or a true friend of a different faith. They'd occasionally had Catholic neighbours, and though their greetings were cordial, it was understood by all that they would not spend many hours together.

For the first time, she seriously considered whether she ought to break off the engagement. She had not yet considered that rather extreme alternative, as she always imagined herself in some happy future where she had found the courage to tell her family and everyone had come to peace with her decision. But that was very far from likely. So far, the engagement had brought her many happy dreams but also much present misery. And she was no longer sure that she could expect anything different.

"Judith?" asked Papa as she sat down with Moses. "I heard you at the door before Mr Barnwell left. Was there something you wished to tell me?"

2

___

Louisa-Margaretta thought of her lost love the moment her carriage came into town. And just as quickly, she decided that she would not think of him. If she spent too much time thinking of the past, she would drive herself mad. And because she had one very important reason for coming to town, she could not afford the distraction.

Like most young ladies, Louisa-Margaretta had been deeply in love with a man she could not reasonably think of marrying. But unlike many, she had gone so far as to form an alliance with him, believing that he would sacrifice his family ties in order to marry her.

Louisa-Margaretta by then knew enough of life to realise that her disappointment, if not universal, was common. She had heard old ladies go on at length about the fancies they'd had when they were younger, laughing about this or that gentleman who would have been a terrible match.

But Louisa-Margaretta could not laugh about Isaac. When he had not answered any of her letters, she had been shocked. It had been a blow that she still could not think on without both anger and shame. Only by living far away and distracting herself with other pursuits was she able to get back some of her old spirits, though she felt that she was a completely different person from the young girl who had eagerly spoken to a handsome young man by claiming a false acquaintance with him while she was in the British Museum. That Louisa-Margaretta was gone, and she imagined that the impulsive and lively young man that Isaac had once been must also have vanished.

She had not gone to London in hope of meeting him. Though she had held on to the idea of a fated match for longer than most young ladies would have, she was not quite so foolish as to question his rejection. All of the letters and messages she had tried to get to him had been unanswered. At great length, she had learned through Judith's friend Letty that he had gone to New York and was not expected back again.

Though she thought of Isaac constantly, she had a more pressing matter to attend to on her trip.

Judith had promised her that they would recover together, in familiar surroundings, as Louisa-Margaretta decided what to do about a man who wished to marry her.

Mr Fortescue was not a pleasant man. Though Judith and Louisa-Margaretta had gone out of their way to help him, he had responded only with threats.

A rich bachelor, he was used to being courted by all of London society. Though he had a terrible reputation as a rake, he had the riches and family background to make many young women, and even their parents, overlook his unsuitable past. Many young ladies in want of a well-provisioned home would have been happy to marry him, and only the richest families in town could afford to turn up their noses at the prospect of one of their daughters marrying such a man. Even those who wanted nothing to do with him were polite. Louisa-Margaretta was the first eligible woman to be rude to the man, and her frankness, along with her beauty, made him long for matrimony as he never had before.

She would have said no, but she had been so unwise as to kiss the man more than once. Not insensible of the very great threat that going beyond kisses would have posed, she did no more, but even that misstep increased her vulnerability and her confusion. For she had enjoyed their meetings, much as she regretted them.

Her visits to Mr Fortescue had consequences that she would never have foreseen. He threatened to tell all of society of her behavior unless she married him, and to spill all he knew of her family's secrets in the process. Her brother Percival, in particular, would have been devastated if Mr Fortescue had shared everything he knew about Peggy, Percival's wife. Though it was generally known that there had been some trouble between Mr Percival Haddington and his wife, the exact nature of what had passed would cause a great scandal if it were to become known more generally. Louisa-Margaretta knew that she had to think of them before she rejected the man, though his threats had cured her of any lingering interest she might have felt in his kisses.

Mr Fortescue had been waiting a whole year for her answer and had told her indirectly, through a message passed along to a friend of Judith, that he did not intend to wait any longer. He had given Miss Haddington plenty of time, and if she did not provide an answer in writing, he would be forced to show himself at Wycliff Castle and demand one in person.

A visit from such a man, Louisa-Margaretta knew, would shatter the peace she had finally found in her new home.

And so she went to town in the heat of summer, when it was at its most unpleasant, as her mother did not trust her to go during the season. Even in summer, she was under Mama's watchful eye, making her wonder whether her mother knew more of what had passed on Louisa-Margaretta's latest sojourn than she had let on.

The first days of their visit felt endless, and only when Louisa-Margaretta heard that one of her mother's oldest friends was in town did she find a way to separate herself.

She woke early in order to have breakfast with Mama. Since her father was away on business, it was only the two of them, and her mother had never favored a late repast.

"Today, we ought to do some proper shopping," said her mother before taking a quick but small bite of her crumpet. "I am sure we do not need to follow every fashion, but you do wear out your gowns so quickly."

Louisa-Margaretta shook her head. "What does it matter what I wear in the country?"

"We have visitors," her mother said. "I'm afraid you cannot just gad about in riding habits, my dear."

"We never have proper visitors at Wycliff Castle," said Louisa-Margaretta. "Only family."

Their location in the wilds of Derbyshire had succeeded in keeping Louisa-Margaretta away from the temptations of London. When her family had first moved her there, it was because she had threatened to elope with Isaac, a Jewish man whose family was equally incensed about the potential union. But Wycliff Castle, while a perfect place to hide, proved rather lonely. Only family had been to visit, and two of Louisa-Margaretta's brothers had yet to see the place. Mama's London friends, who had all sworn that they would love to admire the lakes and peaks of the surrounding country, could never be troubled with the long and arduous journey.

Indeed, that was one reason that Louisa-Margaretta's mother had finally agreed to accompany her daughter to London. Though the summers were unpleasant, and most people with means sought to escape the city, there was still a friend or two who had stayed on. Louisa-Margaretta had spent all of her days being dragged to the homes of those friends with her mother. Though she was adept at nodding politely and trying to stab at the ugly embroidery she carried about in her work bag, she longed for a hunt or at least a long ride. Perhaps she was meant for the country herself.

"I heard that the Countess Koltsova is in town again," she said. "Perhaps you ought to go see her. We could have Augustus back on our shores in a fortnight, even if he still would not come to Wycliff Castle."

Her mother's smile was both nostalgic and sorrowful. "Dearest, we cannot expect to bring your brother home so easily. The life of a diplomat necessitates a great deal of travel."

Louisa-Margaretta took off her gloves. Then, seeing how brown her hands had become, she put them back on. She had started using white cream during her time in London as, for the first time, she found that she hated the way other ladies tittered at her tan fingers. But the cream was not yet having much of an effect.

"Yes, Mama. And the Countess Koltsova has the highest diplomatic connections and few friends left who knew her as little Lilias Dunn."

Mama paused. "You do not wish to see her, I take it?"

"And hear how I was a once disgraceful child and have only grown into a tiresome and disgraced spinster?"

"You are not disgraced, my dear," said Mama sharply. "Your father and I have made sure of that."

What would Mama think if she learned how very close to disgrace the whole family was? Louisa-Margaretta had to go to Mr Fortescue and beg him to relent. Even Augustus, who had surely never had an improper thought in his life, would suffer needlessly if that man made good on his threat. *Can a diplomat weather the scandals that would then come out?* Louisa-Margaretta thought not.

But she needed to convince Mama that she was happy and well, so she smiled as she continued telling her about all the very material advantages that would come from an audience with her old friend.

"It does not mean that Augustus will invite me to stay once he and Lucy-Anne return to London. I'm sure he still finds me dull."

"They may not return for decades," her mother said. "And he does not find you dull. If anything, I'm sure he envies you."

Louisa-Margaretta nearly choked on her tea. "Envies me? He gets to enjoy the entire world while I stay in a little corner of Derbyshire, writing ditties with the one lonely girl who has deigned to befriend me."

Her mother sniffed. "You would do well to find other friends if Miss Judith St Clair's company no longer suits you."

"Mama, you are too hard on Judith," said Louisa-Margaretta. "I did not come back from Essex feeling miserable because she had neglected me. You must realise that."

"We needn't discuss it," said her mother, turning away.

Louisa-Margaretta leaned in, so her mother was forced to look at her.

"But you have hardly said one word to Judith for an entire year."

"I am sure that is not true." Mama stood abruptly. "I will take your suggestion and call on my friend, though I doubt even she will be able to contrive a London posting for our dear Augustus."

"I will await your news," said Louisa-Margaretta, waiting until her mother was out of the room before adding "and I shall enjoy a walk."

The sensation of walking unaccompanied in London was so unfamiliar that she enjoyed it immensely at first. Just being out in the sun, walking along like any other city dweller, was thrilling. Louisa-Margaretta knew that she would attract comment if she were out long unaccompanied, yet she could not bring herself to worry. So many people were gone for the summer, after all. If Mama did get word of it, Louisa-Margaretta could claim she had been out of spirits. Mama thought that nobody was ever so low in spirits as to require anything more than a good walk as a remedy.

It was only when Louisa-Margaretta arrived at Mr Fortescue's door that she remembered her errand and grew cautious.

"What an unexpected pleasure," he said when she was announced, rising to kiss her hand and stare at her with his customary wolfish smile.

"I hope it is not," she said, sitting stiffly in what appeared to be a very fine chair. Mr Fortescue always had money, she had noticed. With some, the money might pass for a reason to marry him, but Louisa-Margaretta recognized it as nothing more than an excuse for evil. Mr Fortescue had decided that he could use people as he liked, and he threw money about instead of atoning for the many sins he had committed in order to earn it.

"Not a pleasure or not unexpected?"

He would parry with her, of course. She noted with some disdain that although he was still handsome, life was beginning to wear on him at last. There were limits to how lovely soulless people could look as they grew older, and perhaps some of his misdeeds were finally expressing themselves in his countenance.

"I have considered your offer," she said.

That, at last, gained his attention. "And? My dear Miss Haddington, do not leave me in suspense."

He truly did seem to be in suspense, which almost touched her. She supposed that, in spite of all of his influence and power, marriage with a person who had little regard for him was the one thing he could not easily obtain.

"And I will continue to consider it," she said. "I cannot allow you to reveal anything untoward about my family, but I am also not capable of immediately accepting your offer."

"A year after it was made? I would hardly call such a thing immediate."

She swallowed. "Many wait longer to marry."

"Like your little friend Miss Judith St Clair?"

"What do you know of Judith?" asked Louisa-Margaretta.

She spoke rashly, and she had cause to repent immediately. She should not have revealed anything. But perhaps it would not have mattered, as Mr Fortescue already seemed to know all.

"I had the greatest pleasure in getting to know her last year," he said, "and I could tell quite easily that she despised me."

"None of this concerns her," said Louisa-Margaretta, but Mr Fortescue went on.

"She has kept that good gentleman waiting for just as long," said Mr Fortescue. "And his reluctance to break with a woman who will not acknowledge him marks him out as a very weak specimen, indeed."

Louisa-Margaretta felt weak. She wanted to fight Mr Fortescue, yet the man held all the cards.

"You cannot know anything of my cousin's life," she said, but it sounded more like a question than she had intended.

He raised his eyebrows. "What? Because we do not move in the same circles? That is true enough. And yet we do find ourselves walking in the same gardens from time to time. If he is so indiscreet as to share delicious little details with his most intimate friends as he walks in a public area, well, I would venture to say that he wishes the world to know."

Louisa-Margaretta breathed again. The thought of her friend's sweetheart having an innocent conversation was less alarming than the idea of Mr Fortescue obtaining that information by worse means. At least he did not appear to have anything in writing.

Louisa-Margaretta strove to keep her voice even. "I am sure you need not compare yourself to anyone. Especially someone who, as you said, does not move in the same circles. He devotes his time to charity work and to study, neither of which would interest you."

"Oh, they interest me. Because I am sure you would not like me to spread word of your friend Miss Saint Clair's thorny little problem."

"And I am sure you would not wish to offend me by doing so," Louisa-Margaretta said.

"If you are quite sure, then that means we are to be married," he said, walking over to her and taking her hand, a gesture that once would have made her tremble but currently disgusted her. She pulled her hand away.

Mr Fortescue did not relinquish it immediately, and for the first time, Louisa-Margaretta felt a frisson of terror. The feeling was not the fear she had been experiencing throughout the visit, of damage to her reputation or, worse, the standing of her family. The sensation was acute and physical, the instinctive response of an animal hunted down.

She responded before she had time to think, snatching her hand away. Mr Fortescue tried to grab it again, but she was ready for him and stood behind the chair, fists clenched.

"I love a woman with spirit," he said. "When is our wedding to be?"

Sincere excitement appeared in his face, and Louisa-Margaretta took delight in taking his triumph away from him. But it was not safe to deny him entirely.

"Not in this season or the next," she said. "Ask me in the spring."

His expression was menacing. "What makes you believe that I will wait six more months for an answer?"

Louisa-Margaretta could not remember why she had come and cursed herself for having gone before Mr Fortescue without a weapon. Each time she spoke with him, he was more conniving and threatening, and she wondered when she would have learned of his true nature had she agreed to marry him right away. Indeed, she had considered it and without Judith's intervention might well have accepted his offer simply to get away from the restrictions and misery that had weighed her down in Wycliff Castle. She was wise enough to know that she knew nothing of true misery. And she realised that being such a man's wife would be an education in that condition.

"I hope you will wait," she said. "But I cannot prevent you from taking another as your wife, if that is your wish."

She tried to smile and could not. She was still hardly breathing and only truly let out her breath once she was blocks away.

3

―――――

Louisa-Margaretta wished that she might seek out a garden, for fresh air called to her spirit. But Mr Fortescue had poisoned that experience with his talk of eavesdropping. She walked until she was exhausted, until her feet ached. Mama was sure to have discovered her absence by then, and since she would be interrogated on the subject of her transgression, she reasoned that it did not matter how long she was out of doors. She might as well be hanged for a sheep as for a lamb.

The sun had made the day hot and dry. Louisa-Margaretta walked to the British Museum. The beauty of times long past was the only thing that could soothe her spirit, and she was drawn to her favourite curiosities like a child in search of sweets.

Louisa-Margaretta easily found Montagu House, where the museum and its collections were kept. She had enjoyed going there even before it became a place where she could meet Isaac. Though as a child she had found museums dull, as a young woman, she thought it delightful to have some modicum of freedom in a public setting. She could leave her chaperone in another room and have a great variety of things in view, just as if she were a man or a respectable widow. Louisa-Margaretta knew in her heart that she should not envy widows, but it was difficult not to imagine herself with the amount of power they enjoyed. *And if one has little regard for one's husband, is it so terrible to imagine controlling one's own time and fortune?*

The gloomy thought came upon her that she might not be allowed frequent visits to Montagu House were she to marry Mr Fortescue. It was yet another reason she ought to reject him completely. And yet instead of counting him one more rash mistake to be left in her girlhood, she was going to be forced to contend with the man. She could not refuse him outright.

She could, however, be refused entry to the museum.

"I am sorry to inform you that the museum is closed," a curt old woman told her before turning away.

"I'm quite sure that it is always open from ten to four on Tuesdays," said Louisa-Margaretta, amazed at the swift dismissal. "Indeed, I have not come lately, but I have been here during those hours in recent years."

"The museum is closed during the months of August and September," said the woman, looking as if Louisa-Margaretta were an imbecile. "But perhaps you were thinking of the Reading Room?"

"Yes," said Louisa-Margaretta hastily, determined to spend at least a few minutes in a building where she had known so many happy days. "Yes, I would be glad to see it."

"This way," said the woman unnecessarily, escorting Louisa-Margaretta to an entrance that she would have easily found. She had never been interested in those rooms before. Inexplicably, she found herself excited to sit in them. Perhaps proximity to good people, to scholars, would help erase some of the sour feeling that was clinging to her after her argument with Mr Fortescue.

The woman stood aside, but she did not leave, which infuriated Louisa-Margaretta. A young man was there as well, and he smiled at both of them.

"I would like use of the Reading Rooms," Louisa-Margaretta said grandly. "One hour ought to be sufficient."

It would not be sufficient, nor was she quite sure that she needed to account for her time, but she thought it was best to pretend that she was familiar with the place.

"Very good, madam," said the man at the door. He was much younger, with flaming-red hair that looked like a pinker, unrulier version of Louisa-Margaretta's own reddish-gold tresses. He had the formality of an old man with all the eagerness to please that could only be found in youth, as his movements were slow and deliberate but his expression sweet and open.

"Thank you," said Louisa-Margaretta, but with an apologetic smile, the young man refused to let her pass.

"Your letter, madam, if you would be so kind?"

"My letter," said Louisa-Margaretta firmly, trying to disguise the fact that she had no idea what the young man meant.

"The one granting you permission to use the room," he said.

She attempted to think quickly. When visiting the museum, Louisa-Margaretta did generally have to write her name down in a particular book for visitors, but she had not required advance permission.

The sour-faced woman took delight in explaining every particular of the rules. She consulted nothing written, but she sounded as if she were reading aloud.

"Persons desirous of admission into this room must

transmit their applications in writing, specifying their names, ranks, professions, and places of abode, accompanied with a recommendation from some person of known and approved character. These, the principal librarian submits to the trustees, who, if they see no objection , will grant an admission for a term not exceeding six months."

"Miss Haddington," said a voice from behind the young man.

"Ah, Mr Rodrigo," twittered the old lady.

The officious woman was different then, her former chill replaced by a distinctly less hostile air. But Louisa-Margaretta could not pay that any mind.

She was conscious only of Isaac's effect on her.

It was a pronounced one. He was looking well, rather tan and wearing an impeccably tied cravat, but that had little to do with the effect. His whole presence inspired in her a joy that was beyond mere giddiness, and she fought to restrain her smile. Without any effort, she would grin so widely that it would split her whole body. She was in her beloved's presence again! He was, at last, there before her.

And he flashed a smile of his own.

"I know it is terribly irregular," he said, "but might I vouch for Miss Haddington's character? Indeed, she was the inspiration for the research I have undertaken, and if I had been wiser, I would have advised her to have everything she might need here for our meeting."

Louisa-Margaretta was breathless when both of the individuals immediately agreed, and she followed Isaac to a table where they whispered across the books like naughty schoolchildren.

"A letter about my character!"

"They can be so strict here and for no good reason."

For a moment, they merely beamed at each other, then Isaac cleared his throat and leaned back ever so slightly.

And Louisa-Margaretta remembered that he had not answered any of her letters. But surely, from the way he made sheep's eyes at her, she could not be mistaken in thinking that he had just as much affection for her as ever! She knew she should not forgive him so easily, but her love for him was inconveniently forgiving. The very fact of that love made her flush.

"I did not know you were in town," she said rather stupidly. "Or that you had come to the Reading Rooms. I came in search of the museum, not knowing it was closed for two months!"

"We always met in spring," he said, and she heard the tenderness in his voice.

"And now you are here, with all these studies of your own"

He touched his neck. "They are not proper studies, really. But I needed to give a reason for coming here, and the books are interesting enough. I much prefer them to social calls or meals at my father's club."

It finally occurred to Louisa-Margaretta, in her stupefied state, to ask what he was doing in town at all. "Do you live in London?"

She saw that he was taken aback by the question and hastened to explain. "I always imagined you living in the country, since you claimed to love the country air," she said, smiling again. At the time, she had teased him and reminded him of all the foul animal smells one might have the pleasure of noticing in the country. But she understood it better now and had even enjoyed the fresh air for something more than hunting or riding.

"I have been in America since we parted," he said. "New York. You never heard?"

"I heard rumors," she said, which was true. But she had expected that the stories referred only to Isaac having been taken away from London in the immediate aftermath of their engagement, not that he had stayed there permanently.

And from the way he looked at her, she could not help imagining the city for herself—what sights she would see, what quaint customs she would come to understand were she to move there. Perhaps there would not even be scandal, as she doubted Mr Fortescue could harm her there.

"And are you going back?" she asked.

He nodded, looking away from her. "I have not been entirely unhappy there. True, when I first arrived, I felt more like an exile than anything, but I have begun to enjoy some things about it. And working for my uncle, I am closer to making my own way, not just sitting about in town, hoping for a medallion."

It had been a subject that occupied them before. Not many Jewish traders were even permitted on the exchange, and the lucky few who had permission, in the form of a medallion, did not wish to give it up. Those fellows were hardly likely to die young or otherwise surrender their lucrative spots, so waiting might be fruitless. Isaac had been anticipating his chance, but he might have waited years without getting it.

"All manner of things are waiting for you back in the colonies," said Louisa-Margaretta, "and you have forgotten London."

"I have not," he protested, his voice loud enough to attract the stares of the other patrons.

"I have not forgotten anything," he said, whispering

again. "Why do you think I bring myself to Montagu House when it is torture for me?"

"Well, then," she hissed, angry that he would profess to remember their London days but decide to run off to New York anyway. *Now, when he could have done as he liked!* After Louisa-Margaretta and Isaac had made the grand mistake of telling their respective families about the secret engagement, she had been kept from his company, and they had never had another conversation.

Never, until that day. But her heart must be lying to her. Clearly, he did not wish to walk outside, find a conveyance, and whisk her off to Gretna Green, though they could have easily enough. Age and experience, instead of making him wiser, had taken away all that was bold in him.

"I must take my leave," she said stiffly. Usually, she could speak quite naturally even when she was furious, but she could not seem to form any words.

"Please listen, Louisa-Margaretta," he said, and his use of her Christian name thrilled her after such a long interval, though it was certainly improper. "I do not attempt to... I must explain. It is not only my profession that awaits me in New York. When I came here after my grandmother's death, I left behind a fiancée."

His pained expression told her how he was feeling, but she would not let his fears be confirmed. She was determined to be cheerful. He did not care for her, and her pride would not allow her to make a show of caring for him.

"Congratulations on your engagement," she said. "Forgive me. I had not heard."

He still looked terrified, but confusion had been added to the mix. "No, why would you have? I thought I ought to let you know. Only, well..."

She could have allowed him more time to explain, could

even have confessed that she was not herself impervious to the temptations of the flesh. And in her case, of the freedom that a marriage might have been able to provide.

But she was determined to leave as quickly as she could. Whispering with such a man in the back of a reading room was a very odd experience, and suddenly, she felt very silly. Isaac was to be married. Of course he did not pine for her! It was madness to mistake his attentive nature for love.

"Please," he said, but she shook her head.

"I hope you will both be very happy," she said.

And she swept out of Montagu House without saying another word.

4

———————

After Montagu House, Louisa-Margaretta went back to Mr Fortescue's home immediately. Since it was later in the day, she was much more likely to be spotted without a chaperone, but she did not care. Appearances were no longer of any concern.

"I will not marry you," she said. "And as for your threats, they disgust me. You, or any of your brothers, may say what you wish about me to your friends. Spread the rumours all about town. I care not one whit."

Instead of the disapproval she craved, she saw that he only smiled.

"You are truly the greatest woman I have ever known," he said. "I am sure that you will not marry me now, but you will eventually."

She did not respond in words. Though the decorative vase next to him tempted her, she left without breaking anything. It was imperative that she leave quickly. Otherwise, she might well end up in tears.

After she arrived at her London home and lied to her mama, Louisa-Margaretta decided that she was ready to leave London. She had been restless before, but at the moment, she paced like a confined tiger. No ride, no long walk through the hills could possibly soothe her, but being denied those things was even worse.

At least she had not shed tears. She was thankful enough for that. Instead, she felt only sadness and a strange sense of dread. Every time she thought she might let her eyes get the least bit damp, she stood and went to another room. The London home was nothing like Wycliff Castle, though, and she found herself going to the same rooms again and again. By the time her mother suggested an outing the next day, Louisa-Margaretta was thrilled by the prospect.

"My dear Lilias wished to see us both today," said Mama. "I do hope you will make an effort to win her over."

Louisa-Margaretta gave only a half smile. "How could I? She's a viper, and she's hated me since I was born."

"You were a rather charming baby," said her mother absently. "She liked you well enough then."

"Mama," groaned Louisa-Margaretta. "You have forgotten the whole charade. You are meant to tell me that your friends would not hate me if only I would make myself agreeable and beg God for forgiveness."

"It is incumbent on all of us to ask the Lord for forgiveness," said Mama. "But we might ask our fellow humans too. That time that you went into my friend's garden, when she had been quite clear that none of us—"

"There was nothing to do in that house, absolutely nothing! I was simply dying of boredom."

"And she had such expectations from that visit, and the lady in question was a marchioness—"

"I wasn't to know. I was seven years old!"

"Well, you could ask her forgiveness or at least pay attention today. I have a sense that there is something very serious that Lilias wishes to discuss with us."

Louisa-Margaretta could feel her spirits lifting the slightest bit. "It is as I thought, then. She is going to bring Augustus back so he might look down his cosmopolitan nose at us all."

Mama shook her head, but she smiled. "If I know my friend, it will be nothing so prosaic."

5

J udith felt that Mr Barnwell should be calling on parishioners on his own, but he begged her assistance with the Chandler family.

"They do not live too far. That is, if we may take the carriage," he said. "Mr St Clair, I will gladly postpone the visit if it will be too much for you."

"I think that would be best," said Judith just as Papa responded, "Certainly not."

The two smiled at each other until Judith nodded, a concession to her father. Papa might not be entirely well, but he had been insisting for weeks that he wished he knew more of what was happening with his flock.

"Miriam will wish to go," said Judith. "Though come to think of it, I have not seen her."

Judith had been cajoling her brothers into giving their mathematics a bit of attention. As soon as that was finished, she persuaded herself that the boys' coats needed mending and altering before winter. It was tedious work, but she could not allow thoughts of Morgan to continually occupy her mind.

"She is already with the Chandlers, I believe," said Papa. "In fact, she is the one who encouraged a visit."

Judith frowned. Miriam did what she considered to be her once-weekly duty cheerfully enough, but in Judith's memory, she never had taken the trouble to identify parishioners who might be in distress.

"That shows some judgement on her part, I should think," she said, and she saw Papa look down.

"Well, my dear," he said, and she peered at him.

"What is it?"

"You know that I can never share something that was said to me about another. Hearsay is as sinful as gossip."

"Of course," said Judith. "But I'm sure Miriam would have told me."

When her father made no reply, Mr Barnwell looked at Judith. "I am afraid there is a good deal of hearsay and gossip about this family flying around the village," he said. "That is why I beg your assistance, Miss St Clair. You will speak to the ladies, and you may judge the situation for yourself."

Judith knew she ought not to ask, but she found it odd that she had not heard any gossip at all about the family.

"Come, Mr Barnwell," she said, standing closer to her father's curate. "Could you not give me any general idea of what I may expect there?"

"Of course," said Mr Barnwell, and he looked so pleased at the prospect that Judith regretted asking.

"No," said Mr St Clair. "I know you are not one to gossip yourself, Judith, but it is best that you go with an open mind. Mr Barnwell and I have been privy to others' talk, but you have not. And that is a blessing."

It was an unusually long speech from Judith's father, and he looked tired as he finished it. Judith wondered again why they were all being forced on a visit that Mr Barnwell was meant to handle himself.

"Very well," she said. "We should go before it gets too late."

And they set out, Judith careful to offer her arm to her father. Mr Barnwell looked as if he would have offered her his arm, and Judith was thankful to be spared. She could imagine few things more awkward than having to cling to the curate's coat on a hot summer day.

Chapter break

"Come in. Come in. It is so terribly hot," said the Countess, clasping her hands and giving Louisa-Margaretta no more than a nod in greeting.

"It is a pleasure to be here again so soon," said Mama. "I suppose that is the way with you, Lilias!"

"I'm sure I don't know what you mean. We may as well go through to the sitting room. It is not always comfortable at this time of day, but we shall survive it."

Louisa-Margaretta struggled not to shrug. She wondered that the woman had wished to see her. How queer that Mama had thought it wise that she join the visit.

"It is your travels I was thinking of," said Mama as they settled themselves in the room, which was both well-appointed and comfortable. "You must go many years without seeing friends and acquaintances then be forced to make up for it when you do come to London."

"They do come see us in Russia and all over the continent," said the Countess, frowning as if she had just eaten a very sour gooseberry. "Young men and their Grand Tours are frightfully extravagant, and yet they must have somewhere to stay. It is really rather trying. One cannot find space for them, not on a diplomat's pay, and yet they come in droves and think nothing of the imposition."

"But they bring stories with them," said Mama. "Surely, that must carry some weight. They entertain you with the outside world while themselves enjoying all that your home, however temporary, has to offer them."

Louisa-Margaretta thought of mentioning that the Countess apparently had at least three homes in Russia that were not temporary at all and probably exceedingly large. But she stayed silent.

"It is rather that sort of matter that I wished to discuss," said the Countess, flashing a look at Louisa-Margaretta that had more skittishness than contempt. "Miss Haddington, your mother was telling me only yesterday that you are unhappy with the society at Wycliff Castle. Rather unvarying, as it is only your neighbours, none of whom move in the same society to which you are accustomed."

Louisa-Margaretta looked at her mother in surprise. Though Mama was as conservative as she could be when it came to the subject of Louisa-Margaretta's potential marriage, posed to reject a suitor on the basis of religion, money, or gossip, she was rather liberal when it came to her friends. She did not pretend to be the social equal of any of their neighbours who lived on estates near Wycliff Castle, and neither did she act as if she were part of the village. But she scorned the society of no one and fairly threw the doors of the place open when it came time for celebrations. She had always insisted that if a queen could dine with the poorest labourer, she ought not to be stingy with her own invitations, and she had made many friends from all sides, even in their short years at Wycliff Castle.

"I was only saying that it can be a bit difficult for a young woman," said Mama, smoothing her skirts. "I was thinking that my friend might know some of the eligible gentlemen here in town. It is high time you were married."

"Mama," said Louisa-Margaretta, prepared to begin her usual speech. For years, she had insisted that if she could not marry Isaac, she would die a spinster. Even when she had been contemplating a marriage with Mr Fortescue, she had still insisted to everyone in her family that she would never marry.

So she would not marry Isaac, but he would be with another. He had discarded her affections in order to take as his bride some woman across the Atlantic. Louisa-Margaretta, who had insisted for years that she was going to remain faithful to Isaac until her death, found her resolve weakening. Surely, she could not think that way any longer. She could not afford to, or her heart would break.

"Louisa-Margaretta," said her mother sharply. "I am sure we do not need to speak of all that now. My friend has called us here for something other than matchmaking."

"Indeed," said the Countess, "though it is matchmaking of a sort."

"Tell us more," said Mama, still looking perfectly easy.

"I have a little problem," said the Countess, "and I need to find the most diplomatic person I know to solve it."

She then told them the story of the Duke of Fordham, who was apparently twenty-third in line for the throne. Very distant, when one considered how many healthy boys were before him, but the disaster with King George was a reminder that anyone might end up being a ruler. No matter how—well, no matter what the circumstances.

The Countess did not say that the Regent was a fool of a monarch, but as the wife of a diplomat, she must have known the truth even more keenly than most Englishmen.

The Duke of Fordham, having no such duties at present, had been trying to have his portrait painted for over a year. It had been some time since it was last done, and he was particularly keen on having himself portrayed in a military uniform. Why he was to be wearing such a uniform rather than engaged in some sort of training or combat was left to the listener's speculation, but Louisa-Margaretta tried to keep her expression polite.

There was a problem with the portraits. Every single one of them was acceptable, though of course some were more to the gentleman's satisfaction than others. In fact, the gentleman still spoke about the ones in which he was posed seated, over his own objections, and portrayed from the knees up. He said that his feet were cut off and he would insist on having the thing done all over again. If not, he would withhold payment.

But it did not matter, because the same thing had happened to that portrait that had happened to all of the rest of them.

It was stolen within a week.

The servants had been interrogated, all of them. After each theft, those living in the house grew more careful until the task of securing the Duke's palatial home each night became so onerous that more servants had to be hired. But the thief did not stop. And there was never enough of a pattern to identify the thief.

The Duke had all sorts of theories about why the thefts were occurring. The Countess thought the culprit must be one of the servants. If the subject of the painting could get away without taking too many of his staff with him, he ought to. Her husband, Count Koltsov, suspected the painters themselves. He thought the Duke ought to select someone with impeccable credentials.

The one thing they agreed upon was the solution. A new portrait would be made, that one as far away as possible, with only a few servants at hand. The painter, of course, would be one who was above suspicion.

And if they agreed, the whole thing would take place at Wycliff Castle.

Louisa-Margaretta's mother beamed. "But of course they must come to us! What a fine thing it would be to have such guests."

"Miss Haddington, what is your own opinion?"

Louisa-Margaretta nodded. "It is my parents' house, and I do not pretend to be the hostess. But if my mother likes the idea, naturally, I agree."

"There is rather more to it than that." The Countess looked down at her cushion as if she had found a pin. She looked back up at Louisa-Margaretta, her eyes narrowing. "We are all, as you can imagine, most anxious for the Duke's comfort."

After a long silence, Louisa-Margaretta said, "Wycliff Castle is by no means lacking in comfort. True, anyone who has the misfortune of staying in a room without a blazing fire may well lose a toe during the night. But we can see to it that the Duke does not suffer that misfortune."

Her reply had not pleased her host, who was looking down.

"There have already been rumours," she said. "Some unscrupulous young ladies fortunate enough to come into the Duke's presence have told the most terrible falsehoods to harm his character after the fact."

Louisa-Margaretta's mother sat straighter and laid a hand on her daughter's arm in an unconscious gesture of protection. "Lilias, might there have been any truth in those stories?"

"No," snapped the Countess. "Certainly not. But it does

require that the Duke stay only in the home of a family in which every young woman has taste and delicacy."

The silence was too long. Instead of asking the Countess whether she might be showing unreasonable favour toward a young man who was, after all, a distant relation, Louisa-Margaretta chose to hear the insult implicit in the older woman's cautions.

"You are saying you do not trust me around this Duke."

The Countess's smile was narrow and insincere. "My dear, I do not intend—"

"Of course you do. But we do not intend to be cast aside as hosts for this gentleman simply because I once had an engagement that was not to your liking."

"It is, well, it is not simply the engagement."

Louisa-Margaretta saw how she must appear to the fashionable set in the *haut ton*. After all, she had once tried to marry a young man who did not share their religion. And she had come dangerously close to disgracing herself with Mr Fortescue, whose reputation did not even do his wicked nature justice.

Countess Koltsova cleared her throat. "Madame Chatel, the painter, is exiled from her home. We also need to be quite sure that her hosts are the right sort of people."

Mama frowned. "Surely, Lilias! Given the professions my sons have chosen—"

"Of course, of course. But it is not only a question of profession. I simply wanted to be sure that all of you would be quite ready to welcome her. How is your French?"

Louisa-Margaretta scowled. "I am sure it is good enough for guests. I shall practise a few fulsome little compliments, and it will not signify whether I understand any bit of the conversation. Indeed, even when I speak English, I am sure I am not expected to understand a great deal."

"Louisa-Margaretta," snapped Mama, who then turned to her friend.

"My dear daughter makes rather too many jokes, but you need not worry. She will be the perfect hostess for the Duke and for this painter. They will be very comfortable with us."

"And the thefts?" breathed the Countess. "Are your servants trustworthy, then?"

Louisa-Margaretta had to smile at that. She knew that her mother hated people who dismissed their servants as untrustworthy, especially without cause.

"Yes," said Mama without rancour. "The painting will be quite safe. Though, really, I hardly know why the Duke has his heart set on a portrait."

Her friend blinked. "Yes, my dear, but all the best families have portraits."

"For a child, I understand," said Mama. "I have a great weakness for miniatures of my children and grandchildren! But why would I care about my own likeness?"

The Countess blinked as if she could not understand. "This, you will need to remember. The Duke cares about his likeness. In fact, I can confidently promise that few things are more important to him."

6

The Chandlers lived in a cottage outside the village, and Judith was surprised that Miriam had been walking there most days without complaint. It felt like a rather long way to go on foot, and Judith blamed Mr Barnwell for not insisting that her father at least come on horseback. Even walking from the rectory to Wycliff Castle could be a trial, especially when the weather was wet or chilly, as it so often was in Derbyshire. The grounds were so extensive that the house was quite far from even its nearest neighbours.

Though Judith looked at her father with some trepidation, lest he tire before they reached their destination, she was glad to see Miriam's cheerful countenance. For years, Miriam had complained about Judith's close friendship with Louisa-Margaretta. Now that she had her own set of friends, she no longer appeared to notice the frequency of Judith's visits to Wycliff Castle.

"Welcome," said Mrs Chandler, a woman Judith vaguely recognized from gatherings at Wycliff Castle. Socially, the Chandlers were recognized as a family of good breeding, but they could not be said to be in possession of a great fortune. Mr Chandler might be a gentleman, but Judith wondered whether anyone in the small cottage might not have preferred that he apply himself to a profession. Her father, though he'd had no choice but to work from a young age, currently enjoyed greater security and purpose than Mr Chandler and his family could boast of.

Introductions were made between Mrs Chandler's daughters and Mr Barnwell, and Judith was thankful for them. She would have forgotten which daughter was which without such a nicety to remind her. One daughter, Cecilia, was upstairs because she was ill.

The other two daughters were Catherine and Caroline to Miriam, who was plainly thrilled to introduce them to her family.

"We are so very pleased to see you," said the elder daughter, Miss Chandler, her smile awkward but not insincere.

Judith realised with a prick of conscience that, because she was keeping house for her father, she ought to have issued an invitation long before. Those young ladies, who were practically strangers to her, were Miriam's bosom friends. And no doubt Miriam had been fed many times during her sojourns there, without Judith offering any Chandler girl so much as a crumb.

They had a pleasant enough conversation when they first sat down, the daughters tittering politely over Mr Barnwell's outraged remarks about the weather. Judith often suspected her father's curate was not quite as loud and opinionated as he made himself out to be, that he put on a facade for his listeners. But if he did, it was a good one, for soon both Miss Chandler and Miss Caroline Chandler were drawn out of their silence.

"One year, it snowed so much I thought we should never be able to leave the house again," said Miss Caroline Chandler with a fond smile at her sister.

A man stepped into the room, his hair windswept, and the ladies all sat a little straighter.

"Mr Barnwell, Mr Chandler," said Judith's father when it became apparent that the man's wife was not going to introduce him. Her face looked sour, and she blinked as she acknowledged her husband.

"I do not know what I would have done that winter if we had been forced to stay in this house much longer," she said, continuing her daughter's story. "Your father must go out, for our own sanity as much as his."

The two Misses Chandler looked away, seeming disappointed at the exchange without being in the least surprised by it.

"Mr Barnwell, Mr St Clair, Miss St Clair, I hope you will forgive me," he said. "I must wash the paint off my hands after my excursion, as you see."

After receiving nods from the guests and still without acknowledging any member of his own family, he left the room.

It was Mr Barnwell who broke the silence, and in doing so, he rose in Judith's estimation. He showed himself to be a man of good breeding when all of the others in the room were wishing for something to say. Even Mr St Clair, whose expertise in soothing ruffled feathers in others' families was extensive, was rather at a loss.

"Your sitting room here is certainly lovely and comfortable," he said. "I imagine that one thinks of such things more in Derbyshire. Some of the London constructions seem to make one colder than outside, if such a thing were possible. Their walls are like parchment."

"Indeed," said Judith hastily. "Though a brisk walk outdoors is often the best way to make such buildings seem less draughty, at least one is out of the wind, or out of the worst of it."

"Well, I, for one, am very happy to have settled in such climes," Mr Barnwell said, addressing himself to Judith when nobody else joined their observations.

Miss Caroline Chandler looked as if she wished to say something, but as she made no sound, she might require more time before joining them.

"They certainly have their charms, if one is fortunate enough to be well provisioned with thick clothing," said Judith.

"Would you wish to stay in Derbyshire, Miss St Clair?" asked Mr Barnwell.

Judith, wary of insulting her hosts, was not sure how to answer. She was saved by Mr Chandler's reappearance.

"Thank you for coming to visit us," he said, settling into a chair that left him in the far corner. Though the room was not large, he was nearly as far away from his family and the visitors as he could be and sitting at such an angle that he would not be able to see his wife at all.

"Yes, Mr Chandler ought to have been here to receive you, but everything is lowered when there is a painting to be got," said Mrs Chandler, and the contempt in her voice was not disguised by any regard for decorum.

Even Mr Barnwell seemed unsure how to respond. For the first time, Judith had the opportunity to observe Miriam, who looked pointedly at their father as if to ensure that he missed none of the exchange.

"Miriam," said Judith, "I believe you left your cloak at home today."

There were stares, confused ones, but Miriam caught Judith's meaning immediately.

"Only you would be cold in this weather," she said. "Mr Barnwell, you will soon learn that my sister is not meant for Derbyshire. Her only virtue is that she avoids the winter so assiduously that she disappears in search of warmth, so one rarely hears her complain."

Mr Barnwell looked surprised and disappointed at that revelation, and Judith felt slighted. *Why should he be sorry about my hatred of the cold when he boasted that he himself is finding it rather hard to bear?* But she was thankful to her sister for interrupting the exchange they had heard.

"Miriam," she said, "I can easily confess to that particular failing, but I am sure our friends are tired of hearing about winter. Might we sing a duet?"

Miriam gave a snort of laughter, which she did not entirely succeed in disguising as a cough. Singing duets was something that both sisters had hated since they were children. Judith had the best ear for music, but she despised performing, and Miriam hated being told what to do. Usually, a sequence happened in which Judith pointed out that Miriam was singing some passage incorrectly, Miriam became offended, and Judith complained to their mother about how impossible it was to accompany someone who could not be corrected. After some years, Judith was allowed to play the pianoforte as Miriam sang, provided she made no attempt to change how her sister was singing.

But the Chandlers had no pianoforte, a fact that Judith was forced to regard as something of a blessing. She and Miriam began a duet they both knew, a rather simple pastoral piece about streams in summer. Though Miriam's chosen key became flatter as they sang, Judith was able to adjust, and they did a couple of songs justice together.

By the time they were finished singing, Mr Chandler had departed the room again, and the visit was drawing to its natural end. Miriam was persuaded to come home with the party, as the sunset was growing earlier each day, and she would surely be cold without her cloak. Judith was glad that she had decided to have the carriage call round for them. They would not have to brave the walk a second time, not when her father still seemed a bit pale and weary.

On the ride home, Mr Barnwell attempted to speak to Miriam about her concerns.

"We can all see Mrs Chandler's unpleasantness," he said. "Thank you for bringing that to our attention."

Judith looked sharply at her father. As far as she was aware, Miriam had taken her concerns only to Papa, and she felt insulted that Papa would feel he could share them with Mr Barnwell and not with Judith.

"We should not speak of it," she said, wondering if she would shame her father. "We do not need to gossip about our neighbours."

"Yes, but what is to be done?" asked Mr Barnwell, ignoring Judith's look of disapproval. "With such a woman, I am sure even the strongest speeches would have little effect."

Papa shook his head. "My child," he said, and Judith nearly choked at how that appellation galled Mr Barnwell, "there is not always something simple for one to do with trouble in a family."

"But, sir, Mrs Chandler—"

"Mr Chandler is far from blameless. As you are well aware, each marriage is comprised of two parties, and when something is awry, it is often the fault of both."

Judith frowned, and Papa continued. "In such cases as these, one must think of the daughters. Do they have the company they need, the cheer to bear the daily difficulties in the home? In this, they are blessed. Thank you, my dear," he said, looking at Miriam.

Mr Barnwell interrupted again. "The daughters, of course," he managed before Miriam spoke up. She did not mind talking over the curate.

"They all paint," she said. "It brings them a great deal of cheer, I believe. But we have not been sketching as much of late. The weather is not fine."

Mr St Clair nodded. "And does their father take an interest in this?"

"Yes, as he does in little else. He is motivated by little other than painting. Caroline says that he treats them the same as he would sons in that he cares only for the art they are able to produce."

"What? For commercial purposes?" asked Mr Barnwell.

Judith laughed quietly.

"Are not paintings rather expensive?" he continued. "Granted, I do not have many friends who are artists, but I also know that I cannot afford to buy such things."

"Indeed, they are a luxury," said Papa. "But I do not think the Chandlers are profiting from their craft."

Judith shook her head. "It would be difficult, though I wonder if it is impossible. And the paintings." She paused. "Miriam, what do you think of the paintings?"

Miriam gave a wide smile. "You mean to ask me whether they are any good, but you are afraid to insult my friends. Catherine's paintings are excellent, very precise, though at times a bit too much so."

"They are too sharp?" asked Judith.

"No, not exactly. The details rendered are always fine, and the colours as accurate as she can make them. Do you understand? There is no romance, no true artistry in it. But she is very technically capable."

"That's rather a harsh thing to say of a friend." Judith could not help scolding her sister.

But Miriam was unconcerned. "Oh, Catherine herself would agree. Caroline's work is more artistic, though the proportions are not always quite right. Cecilia is most like their father. She uses lots of strange ideas to make the oddest things."

"And Mr Chandler?" asked Mr Barnwell.

It was funny that the father himself had been forgotten, but then, it did seem that he wished to disappear. It was as if he were hardly a part of his own family, merely a guest passing through the little rooms of the cottage.

"He tortures himself over the art," said Miriam, preparing to depart from the carriage. She touched her hat. She had just added new ribbons to it the day before, as she always liked to show off the newest fashions she could find, even when there was nobody to appreciate them.

"Tortures?" Papa sounded concerned.

"Oh, spending weeks on one corner of one painting, that sort of thing. None of his art seems very good to me. He certainly cannot rival his daughters."

"He might still sell paintings with the right sort of patron," Mr Barnwell mused. "Might our friend Mrs Haddington be persuaded to take him under her wing?"

"The rich can be unhappy as well," said Papa. "In fact, with more money, Mr Chandler might well find his life much more trying. The eye of the needle, you know."

Mr Barnwell had no response, and Judith and Miriam looked at each other while suppressing sighs of frustration. It was the most companionable exchange they'd had in months. Their father's lectures on the virtues of poverty had always troubled them, as they generally came at the heels of some bitter difficulty to do with money. Papa could simply not see how humiliating their want of funds could be, as he himself never felt envious. But since he had taken a position so well compensated that their earlier penury was only a memory, Judith wondered if he was ashamed of their good fortune. Perhaps he feared being barred from heaven himself.

"We all may help him in our own way," Judith decided. "But Mr Barnwell, if you are able to assist with the sale of the paintings, I think it would mean the world to the family. I would help, but Mrs Haddington hates me."

"She does not hate you, my dear," said Papa gently, shaking his head as they got out of the carriage.

"Strongly dislikes," said Miriam cheerfully.

"Nobody could hate you, Miss St Clair," said Mr Barnwell, and Judith sighed.

"I am not saying that I blame her," she explained. "But I do not think suggestions from me would be well received."

"Well, I am happy to make them," said Mr Barnwell.

Judith looked about. Miriam and her father had gone inside the house without saying goodbye to Mr Barnwell, which was shockingly rude. Unless, perhaps, they assumed that he would follow everyone in and conclude the day by dining with them, as he so often did.

Judith knew she ought to invite him to join them, but she found herself shrinking from the idea. At the end of each day, Judith wished for nothing more than the comfort of being surrounded by her family. Because she was considering marriage, that was even more important to her. If by some miracle Morgan was accepted, and her brothers and father did not renounce her—Miriam would not, Judith thought, but she could not be sure of the others—she would still be leaving them all. Those meals would soon be part of her memory, of a girlhood that had stretched into their Derbyshire years. And she did not like to think that some of their last evenings as a family would be wasted with Mr Barnwell's theological ramblings.

"Good day, Mr Barnwell," she said firmly. "Thank you for your company."

He looked dismayed, but he could hardly reject such a clear dismissal. "Thank you, Miss St Clair."

Judith felt sorry for him as he left in their carriage. It was time for him to go to the room he was renting in the village, and she wondered if he got proper meals there. Nobody had anything good to say of Mrs Knight's cooking. But Judith swallowed the guilt, as she was still glad he had not joined them.

By the time she walked into the house, she had forgotten the guilt over Mr Barnwell and begun anticipating the arrival of her friend. When Louisa-Margaretta finally returned, perhaps they could then do something for the Chandlers.

7

———

Louisa-Margaretta sighed when she sat down at the pianoforte. Eyes wide, she looked at Judith. "Remind me once more of the purpose of all this."

Judith sat down next to her friend, placed her hands over the keys, and began to pick out a familiar Bach invention. Though Louisa-Margaretta liked Judith to invent new melodies, Judith always preferred to begin with something that she loved.

She could tell that Louisa-Margaretta had not shared all of the details of her time in town. In describing Mr Fortescue's tirades, Louisa-Margaretta had suddenly gone quiet. Judith knew there must be more that the man had said, and perhaps her friend would share it if only the balm of music could heal her wounded pride.

"You are not in spirits," said Judith. "And I find music rather more comfortable than riding."

"Why should I be in spirits?" Louisa-Margaretta banged out a hasty chord before turning away. "I am only waiting for doom to befall my whole family."

"I should not worry about Mr Fortescue," said Judith,

resuming the Bach as Louisa-Margaretta began to pace the room.

"You worry more about scandal than I do," said Louisa-Margaretta. "You would be out of your wits with fear if you were in this situation!"

Judith did not mention that she would never be in such a situation. Indeed, she simply could not afford such a lapse. If her secret engagement were discovered before she announced it, there would be scandal enough, though Morgan was well thought of in the neighbourhood. She had responded to her friend's distress with a natural concern and a kind heart, but that did not make her indifferent to the very great chasm that existed between their two situations. Louisa-Margaretta had already caused a great scandal with one engagement, spent time alone with an insufferable rake, and caused her parents heartache and worry for years on end. Judith, who could not seem to bear one unsuitable engagement, could not imagine being so easily swayed by passion.

"I do not believe that he will make good on his threat," said Judith, slowing her playing as she tried to calm her friend. It was a difficult thing to do when she herself had not felt well for weeks. Every day, she worried that Morgan would appear. Instead of greeting him with the warmth of love, she would be forced to bear the shame of her failure.

"He has every reason in the world to spread those rumours," said Louisa-Margaretta. "And they are worse for not being rumours. He could tell any number of truths that would ruin our family."

"But then he would lose the possibility of marrying you," said Judith. "As things stand, you are unmarried, and there is a chance you might change your mind."

Louisa-Margaretta spun around, eyes fiery, and Judith held up a hand.

"I know you will not," she said. "Louisa-Margaretta, I would never allow you to accept such a man. I would barricade my father's church before allowing it, you know I would. But as long as you are a spinster, I truly believe you to be safe."

Louisa-Margaretta sat again on the bench, her anger replaced by desolation. "If I am to be a spinster, at least I shall be a rich one. I can get a house in town and go to the theatre every day if my father or brother is so kind as to provide me with an allowance."

"We can earn," Judith said gently. "Remember, it was dear Morgan who first gave us the idea, and of late, we have done nothing with it."

Louisa-Margaretta gave Judith a sharpish look, and for a moment, Judith worried that they would begin speaking of her engagement. But Louisa-Margaretta wanted to discuss Morgan's little scheme instead.

"The idea of selling music? I have not the first idea of how it is done and no head for business."

"But I have a head for music," said Judith firmly. "And you are brilliant at the words. The business may come later. I am sure it's only mathematics, so I may as well see to those dealings."

Louisa-Margaretta gave a faint smile. "Only mathematics! You say that as if it is nothing at all. I am sure there is nothing so dull as mathematics. But I suppose we may as well write a song, as there is little good that will come of being crossed in love otherwise."

Judith bristled. She did not like to think of herself as crossed in love, though it was certainly true that the path she shared with Morgan was not running smoothly.

"Here, listen," she said. "I have been playing this tune for a fortnight, but I do not know what words ought to go with it."

Louisa-Margaretta listened only once before she began singing, her voice as clear as ever in spite of the turmoil Mr Fortescue had caused in her heart.

I go to bed this evening
With naught but trouble in my heart
I cannot see for weeping
Because we two must part
Our summer days together
Have reached a chilly autumn end
I'm sure that I shall never
Speak words of love again.

Judith laughed in spite of herself. "Louisa-Margaretta, it does not fit the character of the music at all! I took such pains to come up with a droll melody, and these were not the words that I had in mind."

Louisa-Margaretta, at last, was laughing. "But imagine what a good joke it would be!"

Judith tried to look stern but kept smiling. "I'm going to play it again. And try to think of better words this time."

After she had played it through at an even quicker pace, alternately glaring at her friend and moving her head in a jaunty demonstration of the intended character, Louisa-Margaretta began to sing again.

They were interrupted when a woman in a white dress entered with Mrs Haddington.

"Oh, you two must be sisters," the lady said in French.

Mrs Haddington, who was usually the picture of composure, flinched at the words. "This is my daughter," she said, placing her hand on Louisa-Margaretta's shoulder. "And this is the daughter of our rector, Miss Judith St Clair."

Their hostess spoke French with an excellent accent, but Judith wondered whether her understanding of the language might be poor. Perhaps she was finding even the simple introductions rather trying.

"Louisa-Margaretta, Miss St Clair, allow me to present Madame Chatel," Mrs Haddington said in French, hardly looking at Judith.

From the earliest days of Judith's friendship with Louisa-Margaretta, Mrs Haddington had taken the liberty of calling the young woman by her first name. But ever since she had returned from Essex with a shaken and angry Louisa-Margaretta, she was once again Miss St Clair, addressed as a guest but not a true friend. Judith herself longed to explain about Mr Fortescue and some of the other events of Louisa-Margaretta's sojourn. But she could never speak in more than generalities, as she did not dare tell Mrs Haddington more than Louisa-Margaretta had revealed. And so it seemed she was destined to be received with chilly glances in that household.

Madame Chatel, in fact, was rather chilly herself. Though Judith was pleased to see that the famous painter the Duke had engaged was a woman, and a foreigner at that, her feelings quickly changed. A male painter might have been snobbish or rude, but Madame Chatel seemed to feel that she could scold Louisa-Margaretta and Judith as a mother might.

"Why are you two amusing yourselves at the pianoforte?" Madame Chatel asked.

Though Judith had never been abroad, she recognised the lady's French as unmistakably Parisian.

"That dear Countess in London says that you undertake no charitable work, Miss Haddington, and simply rattle about in this castle all day."

"*Comment?*" asked Louisa-Margaretta, a bright smile on her face.

Judith sighed. She knew that while Louisa-Margaretta had been forced to study German and French with various governesses, none of them had been able to discipline her friend. Judith, on the other hand, had learned many languages on her own. Though her parents took the education of their children seriously, with so many children, they could hardly take an active role in Judith's learning. Indeed, even before their mother's death, Judith had been pressed into service as a governess of sorts for all her younger siblings, particularly since most of the learning came easily to her.

"It is an honour to meet you, Madame Chatel," said Judith. She knew that her French, while grammatically accurate, certainly sounded as if it was spoken by a foreigner. She did not have the rhythm of the language right. It sounded halting and shy.

"And you the daughter of a rector," said Madame Chatel. "I am sure you know all about making use of your time."

"I hope I do, Madame," said Judith.

"Then why do the two of you not join me?" asked Madame Chatel. "It would be useful for you to occupy your hours."

Judith, unlike Louisa-Margaretta, was not enamoured of the woman's work. She longed to tell her that she was not in want of ways to occupy her waking hours. Indeed, since her father had not remarried, much of the work that customarily would have fallen to the rector's wife was done by her. Engaging Mr Barnwell as a curate had taken some of the weight off Judith's shoulders, but she still found herself with enough duties to occupy the better part of her days. Though her aunt Leah had insisted that neither Judith nor Miriam ought to try to take their mother's place, there were simply too many responsibilities to leave them all to Papa.

"I would be honoured to help you paint," said Judith. "*Oui, Mademoiselle Haddington?*"

"*Oui,*" said Louisa-Margaretta breathily. From that one word, anyone listening would have thought her the far superior French speaker.

"Excellent," said Madame Chatel. "I used to do three sittings a day. That is, until my friends persuaded me otherwise. I will start the first at dawn. That can be with my fellow guest, the Duke. And after that, Madame Haddington, I will make a start on your portrait."

"I am sure you do not need to paint mine," said Mrs Haddington with a touch of her usual kindness coming back. She was no longer skittish, and her French continued to sound excellent to Judith's ears.

"Nonsense, but I must have you as a subject! You have such spirit. It will make the portrait easy. And such features —they are so classical and even, and such a neck!"

Mrs Haddington laughed heartily. "At my age, I am sure I should not think of my neck."

"Well, everyone who sees the portrait will admire it. That is certain. And your daughter has certainly inherited it," said Madame Chatel, looking at Louisa-Margaretta.

Judith followed her gaze. Louisa-Margaretta was as beautiful as her mother, with the same tall figure and stately proportions. Even when she did not eat well, which was unusual, she did not fade away to a pathetic wisp as Judith did. Lately, with the anticipation of a possible break with her family, Judith could feel her stays growing looser. She knew that she would lose what little bloom she might have left, yet she could not seem to force herself to eat.

There was something of the Haddingtons in Louisa-

Margaretta, and Judith wondered if Madame Chatel would be able to capture it, should she choose the young woman as one of her subjects. Where Mrs Haddington's face was so long that some might have found it rather too narrow, Louisa-Margaretta had the rounder face of her father, though her features were an echo of her mother's. Judith had noticed that she and her brothers all looked different, but when the Haddingtons were together, the familial resemblance was clear. She wondered that none of them were shorter and darker, like their father, but reasoned that he must be rather proud to have such handsome children.

Madame Chatel drew closer to Mrs Haddington. "Now, tell me, how did you find the rector for your little church? I imagine he is the cousin of your husband, non? You English, you have a very charming way of choosing clergy."

Mrs Haddington flinched once again, and Judith registered her reaction with fascination. She was not used to seeing her friend's mother so discomfited. Perhaps Madame Chatel, who was famous not for a family name but for formidable artistic accomplishments, was intimidating to a woman who had always been highly regarded for her elegance, breeding, and warmth.

That was rather ironic, for Judith knew Mrs Haddington had a lively and active mind. She and Louisa-Margaretta both had a great deal of vigor and high spirits, though their interests rarely aligned. And Mrs Haddington, unlike many great ladies, had a spiritual bent that left her unsatisfied with the mere appearance of piety. She prayed with and for everyone about her, sometimes to such a degree that all in her vicinity felt exhausted.

Yet there she was, murmuring her response to Madame Chatel. "No, he is no relation to my husband's family or mine."

She looked at Judith, and her face seemed set in a frown. Judith wondered if Mrs Haddington regretted her words. As angry as she still appeared to be with Judith herself, she had never yet spoken ill of Mr St Clair.

"Though of course, we consider him to be part of the family, in a manner of speaking," said Mrs Haddington. "You will meet him, Madame. I am sure you are tired. Shall we take our tea in the drawing room? I am sure you will enjoy the prospect."

Judith exchanged a glance with Louisa-Margaretta, who appeared equally baffled by that version of her mother. Mrs Haddington was usually just as easy in company as she was with her children. Though Judith imagined that Louisa-Margaretta could understand little of the French, the tremor in her mother's voice was unmistakable.

Madame Chatel replied that she was, indeed, quite hungry, but before they could sit down and eat, they were interrupted by the distant sound of a carriage.

The Duke had arrived.

8

───────

The meal was much delayed by the Duke's arrival, but at length, the company sat down at the formal table. There had been no time for Judith to leave, and Louisa-Margaretta wondered what her friend would make of the guest. She herself felt excited, though her eagerness was tempered by a desire to behave perfectly. At any normal meal, Louisa-Margaretta knew all the rules about a lady's behaviour and chose to ignore many of them. She talked out of turn, took large bites of food, and asked far too many times when the next course was to arrive. Louisa-Margaretta's father often announced with pride that his youngest child was hopelessly spoilt and ate like a peasant.

But that night, Louisa-Margaretta would not allow the Countess to hear anything of her manners. Indeed, she was still thinking of ways to get revenge on her mother's friend. The woman had insulted Louisa-Margaretta, all while asking for a favour! It was not to be tolerated.

Louisa-Margaretta was fortunate enough to be seated next to Mr Galpin, a great friend of the Duke, who had invited himself along with the party. Though she was not seated next to the most honored guest, she was sure that his friend would be sure to report anything clever that she might say.

"This is the most well-traveled group of visitors we have hosted in many months," she said, smiling at Mr Galpin. "I hope you find Derbyshire to your liking."

His mouth was weak, and he looked at her as if she could not believe what she was saying, causing her to blush in spite of herself.

"There are many beauties here in Derbyshire," he said. "But the weather is abysmal. If not for the company, I would have insisted that we return immediately."

She gave a hesitant smile in return. "Then I hope you find the company to your liking."

Mr Galpin nodded. "I am sure that we shall."

Louisa-Margaretta turned back to her place setting and her first course. Mr Galpin reminded her of Mr Fortescue in some way. He had gazed upon her only while they were speaking, which was perfectly permissible, but there was something threatening in his gaze that caused her to wish him far away from her home. With Mr Fortescue, it had been different, at least at first. Louisa-Margaretta had been drawn to him, so she felt both pleased and alarmed by his attentions. But that man was different. Unlike the Duke, he did not have the benefit of anything pleasing in his countenance, and he and Louisa-Margaretta had only just been introduced. Yet he was speaking to her as if their acquaintance was a much longer one.

She observed him closely during the next course as he spoke to Mademoiselle Chatel. His French was impeccable, but she was no less concerned for the young woman who sat on Mr Galpin's other side.

"I am happy to defend my friend's property, of course,"

he was saying. "He wanted a portrait. He shall get a portrait. But to my mind, portraits of beautiful ladies are much more worth our attention."

Mademoiselle Chatel blinked, looking from her mother to Mrs Haddington but finding no ally at the table. All of the other ladies were too far away from Mr Galpin to hear what he was saying, and since he was speaking in French, he might have assumed that Louisa-Margaretta could not hear him either.

Louisa-Margaretta should have waited for the next course to turn, but she rarely observed those niceties, even in company. She was forever being reprimanded by her mother for interrupting other conversations.

"Mademoiselle Chatel," she said. "I do hope you find England to your liking."

Mr Galpin looked bemused. The young woman looked at her mother then at Louisa-Margaretta, appearing unsure of whether she ought to answer.

"It is rather cold," said Mademoiselle Chatel. "But your home is quite comfortable, Miss Haddington."

"Yes, indeed," said Mr Galpin.

"My dear," said Mrs Haddington to her daughter, her stern eyes at odds with the apparent warmth of her smile, "I am sure you shall get a chance to speak to all our dear guests in due course."

"Yes, Mama," said Louisa-Margaretta, turning back to her food. The courses seemed exceptionally slow. Whenever they did not have company, Louisa-Margaretta and her father ate quickly. Mama was forever despairing of the pace of their dinners, which she found rather coarse.

When the ladies and gentlemen separated after dinner, Louisa-Margaretta rushed over to her friend. Though she had been uncomfortable in the presence of the Duke and his friend, she was very curious about the intrigue surrounding her home.

"Do you have a sense of the thief, Judith?" she asked as soon as she was certain that their soft voices would not be overheard.

"No," murmured Judith. "But the Duke would not stop going on about the prettiness of the countryside here. He seems to prefer carriage rides to hunting, though."

Louisa-Margaretta scoffed. "Mama would not let me hunt with the men, at any rate. I am supposed to be perfectly demure during their visit. I suppose it will be a welcome distraction from all that has passed with my friend."

Judith pressed Louisa-Margaretta's hand. The latter had said almost nothing about how poorly she had slept since her return from London, how devastated her brief moments with Isaac still made her feel. But she felt certain that Judith knew. That heartbreak had been years in the making, and Louisa-Margaretta was not certain that she would ever recover.

Judith cleared her throat delicately. "Well, then," she said. "You may act like a perfect lady, if you wish, and in the meantime, we will solve this matter of thievery. My first guess, if I had to make one—"

She was interrupted by a servant, who acknowledged her before addressing Mrs Haddington.

"If you please, ma'am, Mr St Clair has sent for his daughter."

"I will order the carriage," said Mrs Haddington. "Louisa-Margaretta, come sit with me."

With dread in her heart, Louisa-Margaretta complied. Since her only friend was leaving, she would have few amusements.

"Come back soon," she told Judith, fighting to keep desperation out of her tone. "Come and see us tomorrow."

Judith gave a quick look at Mrs Haddington and a smile that Louisa-Margaretta recognised as pained.

"Thank you for the invitation, Miss Haddington. I will speak with my father."

9

———

J udith's father, for all his attention to the church, was not entirely ignorant of the activities of his daughters. He knew that his duty was to play the role of both parents, and while he could never be as extravagantly joyful or as unfailingly attentive as his late wife, he did try to ensure that his daughters ate well and were in generally good spirits.

With Miriam, he had no trouble. Ever since her aunt's latest visit, the general feeling was that she was much improved. She walked every morning, took pains over her toilette, and accompanied her father on visits to his parishioners at least once a week. For the first time since their move to the neighbourhood, she had friends. Though she was little interested in literature or art, Miriam read poetry and made passable sketches in order to share that experience with other young women.

Indeed, at times, Judith was jealous of her sister. Louisa-Margaretta remained Judith's only true friend in the neighbourhood, and she often felt that both of them might have done better had they stayed in Essex. But Louisa-Margaretta had needed the solitude and safety of Derbyshire when Mr Fortescue was pursuing her, and so Judith returned home as well.

Since Judith's only friend was a difficult young woman who shot birds and rode to hounds with indecent enthusiasm, her social calendar was very simple. Most of the time, she was free to help Papa with his duties or oversee the studies of her young brothers. Occasionally, she stayed over at Wycliff Castle, and when she was not nearly living there, she was a frequent guest, in spite of Mrs Haddington's unvoiced disapprobation. Judith thought that when she requested a few days there, her papa would say nothing, and she was surprised when he tried to stop her going.

"Not with the company they already have, Judith. I will not have you inconveniencing my patrons."

Judith frowned. Though her father was often exhausted by Mrs Haddington's enthusiasm, he had never referred to her as simply a patron. From the very first, the two had had a sincere regard for each other, and Judith had even tried not to let her father know that she had recently fallen in the good lady's estimation. She had failed, of course. Village gossip was swifter and sharper than anything one might see in London, and there was probably not a single soul in the village who did not know that Mrs Haddington was displeased with her daughter's only friend.

"I was invited, Papa," she said. "And Madame Chatel has asked for my help. Louisa-Margaretta can assist her during some of her sittings."

"With the Duke?" her father asked, and Judith was shocked to hear the edge in his voice. "That would not be proper, and I will not allow it."

"Papa," she said, but he shook his head.

He did not raise his voice above a normal level, but he

had a bit of iron in his response. "Judith, I am surprised that you would ask again. You are needed here. Miriam requires you, as well as your brothers, and Mr Barnwell has been constantly asking for your assistance."

Privately, Judith thought that Mr Barnwell ought to learn to be independent. Indeed, he had been hired to help relieve the burden on the St Clair family, not add to it by way of a constant need for tutelage. But she said nothing, so surprised was she by her father's outburst. Well, for the rector, it was an outburst. In anyone else, it would have been considered no more than a cross word.

He sighed. "I have not expressed my position very elegantly, my dear. Your mother would have done it better."

Judith found herself temporarily unable to speak, blinded by the thought of Mama. Indeed, she had been thinking of her mother even more than usual of late. The grief was growing worse, not abating, and Judith thought all of the promises about the passage of time soothing her heart must have been lies. True, her feelings for Morgan and the events she had witnessed in Essex had distracted her, but since she was faced with the prospect of being barred from her own family, she thought of her mother with a constant gnawing sense of guilt.

"Papa," said Judith, softening. Though she could not agree with her father, at least she could acknowledge the person who filled their thoughts. "There is nothing wrong with how you expressed yourself."

"You are no longer a child," he said. "And I respect your experience and wisdom, Judith. But I must beg you to trust my understanding."

"Yes, Papa," said Judith, and that might have been the end of it.

But in her heart, Judith was not prepared to yield, and

she resolved to settle on some stratagem that would allow her to be near her friend.

For if she did not, she would be forced to spend the coming weeks quite alone, bearing the burden of her failure with no confidante. If she did not have company, her shame would crush her.

10

Papa had always worked all hours. Mama used to tease him, telling him that working in the night was a luxury that a mother could ill afford. After all, she could not be dozing about in a pew or a library during the day, not when the children needed her. And though Papa could not be said to have shirked any of his duties, he often went to sleep so late and rose so early that his eyes would close of their own accord in the afternoon.

Since his illness, though, the rector had required more rest. For months, he had tried to work as if he were still well, harder than most young clergymen. Judith had finally begged Louisa-Margaretta to intervene. The latter wrote a letter to her cousin, a physician who asked pointedly whether Mr St Clair thought his children would benefit from the early death of their only living parent. After that, Mr St Clair resolved to work with his body's limitations, not against them, though that went sorely against the grain at first.

And so it happened that Papa was still sleeping after Judith finished a hasty breakfast. She went over to Wycliff

Castle before he could forbid it, telling herself that she would get Louisa-Margaretta out for a ride. Although Judith hated the stables almost as much as she despised wobbling about on one of the "gentle" horses, she knew that her friend's spirits were never impervious to a brisk trot on a chilly morning. Judith could spend an hour with Louisa-Margaretta while hardly breaking her promise to Papa. After all, if they were merely riding about the grounds, she would not be disturbing the household.

But Judith had forgotten how much her friend loved sleep. She found Louisa-Margaretta still abed, but she was shown into the breakfast room before she could bow out of the call entirely.

"You are late" came a voice from the far corner. "Come here at once, or we will miss the best light of the morning."

Because the words were spoken in French, Judith took a moment to think of what they must mean. Mrs Haddington wore an elegant green gown, posed against a column with some of the few wildflowers that were still blooming so late in the year.

"Thank you, Miss St Clair," said the painting's subject, her expression of calm repose broken by a frown.

"Madame Chatel," she called in French, "might your daughter not assist us? I am sure she has more experience in such matters than Miss St Clair."

Judith knew the sentence was not designed to provoke her, but she felt a flash of temper. She had lost sleep over the pathetic state of Louisa-Margaretta's heart then rushed over to the large home to provide her friend with the best possible salve. And her loving mother, who might have been at least a little bit thankful for those efforts, was instead brusque and snobbish.

"I am perfectly capable of assisting Madame Chatel," she said, unsmiling. "What may I do first for you, Madame?"

The painter, dressed in white and peering determinedly at her subject, inclined her head gently. "My brush. The smaller one."

Judith looked at the lady's extensive collection of paint-brushes, hesitating over the choice.

"Quickly," snapped Madame Chatel, and Judith chose two. The painter barely looked at one before snapping it out of Judith's hands.

Judith was irritated at being treated like a servant, but she could not help but admire the talent she was witnessing. Though it was hardly light outside, no fewer than three sketches lay discarded next to the canvas. Madame Chatel had already begun to grow decisive in her efforts, and the scene was recognizable. Judith wondered if it would be a flattering portrait, as Madame Chatel was known for, or if there might be some elements of truth in the face she portrayed. Mrs Haddington was not looking well that morning, though with Madame Chatel, Mrs Haddington was polite, even animated. Something about her face looked suddenly older. Mrs Haddington had always given the impression of a very young woman transported into the body of a respectable matriarch, but that day, her grey hairs had multiplied, the folds in her face no longer quite overtaken by her youthful enthusiasm.

"I am sure you have devoted quite enough time to my sitting," said Mrs Haddington. "I am afraid I must have distracted you by chattering on in this manner. Had you not better prepare for the primary subject?"

Madame Chatel shook her head. "That canvas will be stolen, I am sure, so what is the point?"

Judith stifled a smile, but Mrs Haddington was not at all amused.

"I am sure whoever was taking them in town could not possibly have followed the Duke to Derbyshire."

"Pah," said the painter. "Anyone could come here. One coach, another coach, and the journey is at its end. There is a lot of trouble with the time, this is true, but it is not complicated."

"A stranger might stand out on the village," said Judith, glancing hopefully at her hostess.

Mrs Haddington nodded so forcefully that Madame Chatel let out a sigh of disapproval.

"And we are all on alert here," said Mrs Haddington. "Nobody unknown to us has been brought in for the visit, and the doors to the castle are all carefully watched or kept locked."

"Keep your head still, Madame. Thank you. So many doors, so many windows! The painting will be stolen. But your portrait may be spared, so I shall make it a glorious one."

"I wonder..." said Mrs Haddington, then she broke off as her daughter entered the room. "Louisa-Margaretta, dear, are you well?"

"Madame, if you please," said Madame Chatel, sounding a bit rude for the first time that morning. "I am sorry. I must be permitted to work. Not everyone may have the easy life of waking so late in the morning, though I daresay your daughter and her friend expect nothing else at this time."

Mrs Haddington gave an indulgent smile. In fact, though she had often tried to wake her own daughter earlier in the day, after Louisa-Margaretta last came back to Wycliff Castle, Mrs Haddington had given up the battle. Louisa-Margaretta had rightly pointed out to her mother that, at her age, it was unseemly for her and her mother to argue over the hour of her waking. Then she had made such a point of it that Mrs Haddington, who had woken all of her sons early each morning over their every complaint, had quite despaired of her daughter.

Madame Chatel cleared her throat. "Miss St Clair, that brush that you are holding."

Judith hurried to give it to her.

Louisa-Margaretta nodded. "Good morning, everyone. Miss St Clair, may I speak to you?"

"I am sorry. We are rather occupied with this," said Judith. She knew that if she rushed off during the time she had promised to help, Mrs Haddington would be angry. "Perhaps a bit later?"

Louisa-Margaretta's glance was full of fire. "Very well. I shall go for a walk on my own."

And she walked out quickly, without another parting word, before Judith could stop her.

11

───────

Louisa-Margaretta found all of the old sketching things that she could before taking off, out into the hills at the back of Wycliff Castle, which she knew well from her habit of riding there.

It was not enough to only walk into the hills. She had to go until she was next to the lake. If it were a warmer day, she would have skipped stones across the water, but her hands were chilly even with all of the exercise. They were certainly too cold for Louisa-Margaretta to bother with sketching, an "amusement" she had never enjoyed.

She realised that there was someone about who did seem to enjoy it. A painter stood at the edge of the lake, clutching his palette with frantic energy, muttering as he looked out at the water.

Louisa-Margaretta could not help sighing. Wycliff Castle was to be beset with painters, apparently.

"You are on our grounds," she said. "This is not a place for painting."

"It is a place created by God," he said. "Do you imagine

that you can possess such a vista, particularly if you do not have the eye to appreciate it?"

Louisa-Margaretta stared at him in shock. She realised that she knew him by sight, though it had been some time since they had spoken. "I beg your pardon. Mr Chatham, is it?"

"Chandler. A pleasure to see you, Miss Haddington."

She stared at the man. Though they had been introduced at balls and in the village, he looked very different that day. His clothing was shabby, spattered with paint, and his canvas had a scene that seemed to bear little resemblance to the lake in front of them.

"Well, Mr Chandler," she said, "I have brought my sketching things. So you should not claim that I have no appreciation for this place."

He softened. "You mean to sketch?"

She nodded. "But my hands are cold. I will come tomorrow a bit earlier. That way, I may make a fire and warm them."

She felt like an imposter. Grabbing her sorry tools, she put them back in the cloth she had used to carry them. It was easy enough to tell Mama and Madame Chatel that she was going out to sketch, but if she were to draw even one line in front of Mr Chandler, he would know that her desire was not sincere.

Her desire for sketching, that was. Though she felt disloyal to Isaac for even thinking it, she noticed that Mr Chandler looked bold and rather dashing. Though he was older than she, he was far from ancient. His dark hair was rumpled, his fair skin pink and glowing from the air. He had plainly not bothered to shave, and she wondered what his cheek would feel like against her own.

Louisa-Margaretta looked away. Those sorts of feelings had caused her no end of trouble, first with Isaac then with Mr Fortescue. She must not allow herself to indulge them, else she might find herself the victim of a fate even worse than a broken engagement or a protracted exile in Derbyshire.

"I must go," she said. "I wish you the best of luck with your efforts."

"When will I see you again?" he asked. "I must paint your portrait."

Louisa-Margaretta had heard many gentlemen ask after her with urgency, and it always amused her. But that man was different. He had an intensity to his manner she could not understand, and she was not sure if he was taken in by her beauty for its own sake or simply eager to preserve it on a canvas. He was staring at her, to be sure, but for what purpose? His eyes had a daring nature, a hunger that was not present in his words, which had been polite enough up to that moment.

She shivered. "Soon," she said. "I come to this point on the lake often. To sketch."

At that, he gave a faint smile. "I have been here three weeks and will be here many more. And I passed this way in summer. Yet I have never happened to see you."

"Well, you may pass this way again if you like," said Louisa-Margaretta, flushing at having her falsehood exposed so easily. "If anyone gives you trouble, tell them to speak with me directly."

He touched his hat, and she could not tell if the gesture was respectful or mocking. "Of course. I shall."

12

Madame Chatel had taken only a few minutes for a cup of tea and a sandwich when she was informed that the Duke was ready. She insisted that Mrs Haddington and Judith accompany her to the room where he waited, and as they walked in the passage, she spoke of what she intended to capture.

"We could wait," said Mrs Haddington, her brisk steps matching the painter's.

Judith struggled to keep up with them.

"Goodness, no! We may as well go ahead. It is not such beautiful light, but then, this painting's life will not be long," Madame Chatel replied, a distant smile on her face.

Mrs Haddington, on the verge of entering the room where the Duke waited for them, hesitated.

"I do wish you would stop saying that," she said, her voice respectful but firm.

"And I wish it were not true! Alas, I have said farewell to many of my paintings. If it pleases you, Madame, I will be sure not to shirk my duty this time."

Mrs Haddington shook her head. "Of course not. I would never accuse you of such a thing."

"Good," said Madame Chatel. "You might ring for a servant, then. I will need some of the brushes that I set aside earlier."

They all entered the room and greeted the Duke. There was a flurry of activity as Madame Chatel helped him stand properly, just as she liked, one of his hands resting on a chair in front of him. Mrs Haddington rang for a maid to get the brushes, and Judith stood at the side. Mrs Haddington was called down to the kitchens to give her opinion on that day's meals, so Judith stood waiting as Madame Chatel prepared her canvas.

"You must be particular about your brushes," said the Duke. "But it's a poor carpenter who blames his tools, ha!"

He winked at both ladies but received no laughter in return.

"She will not fetch the right ones," said Madame Chatel, and her annoyance was visible. "I will have to go show her. Silly girl. You, come with me."

That last bit was said to Judith, and the Duke walked over to where she was standing.

"Certainly not," he said, and he stood so close to Judith that she could hardly believe he was not touching her. "Miss St Clair can stay and entertain me while you polish your instruments."

Madame Chatel looked at them, her eyes narrowing. "I would rather have her assistance," she said, smiling though her voice was anything but warm. "Or perhaps that of your friend Mr Galpin. I could summon him. Do you know that when I was in Russia, we summoned the servants by clapping our hands, not ringing? Just as if we were in a harem!"

"Truly, Madame," said the Duke. "Do not trouble yourself."

"I will be only a minute," she said, looking rather vexed for the first time that Judith had seen.

As soon as she left, the Duke moved from his place and walked over to Judith. "She says she will not be gone long," he said, and Judith briefly wondered why he was speaking French. "But she may be delayed."

At that, he reached for Judith's waist with one hand and placed the other on her back before drawing her to him for a kiss.

Her body responded before her mind could follow. Judith had never been fond of exercise, though she was often obliged to walk, and she did not consider herself strong or particularly nimble. But many days, when her brothers were suffering from want of activity, she was forced to join them behind their home. Miriam would play for some time, but she would find their games dull, and only Judith was interested enough in the outcome to stay. She did not always enjoy the games, either, but after their mother's death, she felt responsible for making sure her brothers got plenty of fresh air during the day. If they wore themselves out, they would sleep well at night and behave decently before any company.

One of the games her brothers loved to play was a simple one involving each participant trying to force the other to the ground. As her brothers grew, Judith had been forced to develop her technique when she could no longer rely on her size in the game. And so she knew how to swing her leg at one of her brother's, forcing him to lose his balance so that she might grab his coat and shove him roughly to the ground.

That was what she found her body doing after the Duke grabbed her. Though his touch left no doubt as to his intentions, he was not nimble enough to prevent Judith from throwing him to the floor.

There was a moment when he only stared at her in shock, and Judith was frozen in terror. But even without breathing, she found her feet moving her back, toward the open door and safety of the passage outside.

Madame Chatel waltzed into the room. "I have everything here. I was quite sure that I had brought all of my brushes, and yet the ones I knew that I needed were still in my room."

Judith made no response, as she could not speak, but the Duke, who had just gotten up and begun to approach her again, smiled with such ease Judith wondered if she had imagined the entire incident.

"Of course," he said. "I am at your service, Madame."

He went back to his pose, and Judith went over to Madame Chatel. The Duke stared at her with a mixture of hunger and amusement, and Judith felt that she might very well be sick.

"My dear Duke," said Madame Chatel, her voice cloying. "If you would, please. I am just putting in the eyes."

"Of course," he said and resumed his former posture of gazing thoughtfully at the window.

"Mademoiselle St Clair, I no longer require you," said Madame Chatel. "I am sorry, but I must have my own daughter. She has much more experience in these matters. If you continue to assist me, things will go more slowly."

Judith felt another lurch at the denigration of her offers of help, but she was only too thankful to leave the room. She murmured, "Of course," and tried to force her features into a smile as she left.

As soon as she was outside the room, she was not sick, but she did lose her ability to stand. She sank to the floor, fearing that she would cease to breathe, and stood only when quiet footsteps let her know that she would be discovered if she did not stand.

13

Judith shivered as she walked through Wycliff Castle. If she could not find Louisa-Margaretta, she would go immediately home after asking a servant to fetch Mademoiselle Marie Chatel. She could not help different thoughts flitting through her mind. If only she had not allowed herself to be alone with the Duke! She now saw through Madame Chatel's hesitation, recognising it as the failed attempt to protect a young woman from a man who was used to having his way with everything.

Judith had heard plenty of stories, both the whispered ones and the things that her mother would tell her directly. Once, Mama and one of the richest ladies of their neighbourhood had had a rather bitter argument over a young girl who was seeking a hasty marriage. The visiting lady, whose name Judith could not remember, had insisted that the young woman should not be allowed to marry in their parish, and Mama was rather straightforward about describing the circumstances under which the girl had fallen pregnant. Typically, she might have been as direct with a friend but not with a guest and especially not in front of her young daughters.

"If you or I were to be violated in that manner, I am sure we would say that the blessing of having the child born to a caring father should not be torn away," she said. "I hardly think taking such a thing from a young girl is our place. If I were deciding the fate of the natural father, I would think hanging far too good. I would much rather see him drawn and quartered or something equally mediaeval."

The Duke had surely not intended to father a child, Judith believed. But then, nobody she had ever encountered had dared to grab her in such a reckless manner. With her brothers, their horseplay was never a surprise.

Or perhaps such fights were at an end. She realised, still shaking from the encounter, that she had no desire to ever play such a game with one of her brothers again. They would have to lose her as a companion. She was more willing to play indoor games, but Miriam was the most amusing as a companion. Judith was always begging them to play more quietly, and if not for their insistence, she would never have learned how to throw off any attacker.

She was in one of the quieter passages of Wycliff Castle, vaguely realising that she was no longer even seeking her friend, breathing too quickly. The library was open, and Judith knew that it must be the place of solace she was seeking. Although there had once been a horrible death there, the room itself had not suffered, and Judith had only to trace the spines of the books that lined the walls before feeling at ease.

Choosing one book was impossible, but Judith stood before the shelves and, under her breath, read the titles. The memories of the wisdom and stories they contained were enough. Though her father was constantly immersed in theological study, and Judith preferred history and novels in foreign languages, their own collection of books was comparatively modest. Unlike the Haddingtons, they could not afford to own volumes that they would never read. The books they did have were well loved and in many instances lovingly repaired.

She was not alone in the library for long. When the shadow of a man passed by the door, she froze in fear, but on seeing Morgan, she blinked in surprise, opening her arms as he rushed to embrace her.

When they first began to speak, both blushing from the unexpected but by no means unpleasurable encounter, they kept hold of each other.

"Oh, how I have missed you," she said, staring into his eyes as if she could make up for the many lonely months.

"I was beginning to wonder," he said in a tone that should have been teasing, only he could not quite manage it. His voice faltered.

She shook her head. "I wrote to you. My words should have left you in no doubt."

"That is the position of your friend Letty," he said, allowing her to slip from his arms. "She told me that you only wanted time to seek your father's blessing."

"Not only my father's," said Judith, feeling cold and weak without Morgan, who had taken a half step back as he looked at her. "My whole family's."

"It is not likely they will all agree, even if your father gives his consent."

Judith bit her lower lip. The terror of her encounter with the Duke had left her weak, and she held the back of a chair. "I know," she said, her voice curt. She would have been able to express herself elegantly if she had not had to fight the man off, but she was suddenly so tired she could have slept on the floor of the cold library.

"Then you must decide, Judith," he said, and she heard that he was also weary. His eyes, normally attentive and vibrant, searched hers. "I cannot keep waiting."

She gasped. "But you promised!"

And indeed, he had. When they had first come to an understanding, he had said that he had no idea of marrying any other woman. He had been so romantic as to suggest that if Judith did not marry him, he would not marry at all. Judith, who had secretly reached an identical resolution, could not help feeling pleased and flattered when he expressed such unfashionable thoughts aloud.

Apparently, he was ready to abandon them. Judith did not think that waiting one year had been such a great trial. After all, many engagements lasted longer, at least when there was a compelling reason that the couple should not marry immediately. But Louisa-Margaretta's judgement had ended up being sound in the end. She had insisted that Judith ought to marry Morgan immediately, and when Judith had hesitated, Louisa-Margaretta mocked her. But at the moment, Judith was facing the sorry consequences of her own timidity.

Blinking back tears, she looked away from her beloved. "I must go home."

"Judith," he said. "I am so sorry."

"No. It is only that I promised Papa. I really should not have come at all."

"Judith," he said, but she was already out of the room, hoping that he would not sense the tears that threatened to overwhelm her.

14

J udith was halfway down the walk when she heard
Louisa-Margaretta calling her.

For a moment, she was tempted to ignore the
voice. Judith needed the walk to the rectory to be
quiet and peaceful if she were to compose herself. She
would need to offer excuses to her father for having been at
Wycliff Castle in the first place, listen to the boys' tales
about their afternoon, and put on her most cheerful expression. Miriam, though she spent little time with Judith,
would know at once if her sister happened to be out of spirits. If Judith meant to fool her, she needed to dig deep into
her soul and find some source of cheer.

But she could not turn away from temptation in the
form of the one person in Wycliff Castle who knew about
her engagement. She kept her eyes away from her friend as
she admitted the truth.

"Morgan came to visit," she said.

Louisa-Margaretta only smiled. "Well, then. You should
get everything settled. Why do you look so pitiful, Judith?"

Judith took out her worn handkerchief, patting her eyes. "He will not accept more of a delay and says that he will marry another if I do not decide to marry him now," she said.

Louisa-Margaretta shook her head. "That is rather arrogant of him, is it not? He cannot know what sort of woman will accept him unless he has already proposed to another."

Judith looked at Louisa-Margaretta, her face empty. When she recalled her would-be fiancé, she saw only the handsomest, most brilliant man, and it was very strange indeed to think of any woman rejecting him. But Louisa-Margaretta, while fond of her cousin, was not above mocking what she saw as his folly. She had never understood his choice of religion, and she had always considered his lack of a profession a profound waste. "He could do a great deal more than haunt drawing rooms, as I must," she had told Judith. Then, when Morgan had announced his intention of studying law, Louisa-Margaretta had mocked him for choosing "the only way to spend one's days that is duller than being a clergyman."

"I am not sure I can bear it any longer," said Judith. "I'm going to end up sending him away. I will not abandon my family."

"Do you have any sense of what it means to have a husband who cares for your well-being, not just some man who sees you as a pretty young maiden who has the good fortune not to be overburdened by wits?" asked Louisa-Margaretta, and Judith started.

They were near the rectory, where she could see her father and Mr Barnwell in deep conversation through the window, but she had forgotten to warn her friend. She needed to find some way of communicating what had happened to the young ladies at Wycliff Castle, for their own safety.

"That way of viewing a young woman, Louisa-Margaretta. Did you have one particular person in mind who ascribes to it?"

She wondered if perhaps Louisa-Margaretta had already fallen prey to the Duke. In many ways, Louisa-Margaretta was less protected. If she did make an accusation against such a man, many people would believe that she had somehow drawn him in. Her history was known to the neighbourhood, not only because gossip was common but also because it was hard to explain a family like the Haddingtons choosing to purchase Wycliff Castle. They had no connections in the immediate area, though her father had business interests in Manchester, and it was quite far from all of Louisa-Margaretta's brothers. Still, Judith knew that when the neighbours heard that Louisa-Margaretta was being removed from the company of an unsuitable young man, they generally felt some sympathy for her parents, even if they looked unkindly on a young woman who would attempt to form such an alliance in the first place. She had not yet lost her footing in society, though she could not afford a great many missteps.

Louisa-Margaretta shook her head, but her lips were pursed. Judith could not read her expression.

"No particular person," she said. "They all view us that way, I believe."

"And have you anything to fear?" Judith began, then she paused. She wanted to ask about the Duke directly, but she could not bear to speak of what had happened. And for all she knew, she had violated some code of the very rich when she agreed to be in the same room as the man, especially without the watchful eyes of Madame Chatel. Perhaps, in not insisting that she follow the painter out, she had issued what the Duke had interpreted as an amorous invitation. If his only fault was in misreading the intentions of an unworldly spinster, surely she should not slander him.

She thought of his look of shock then anger when he got up from the floor and walked in her direction. If Madame Chatel had not come in, she could not answer for what would have happened. Some part of her mind told her that a man with honourable intentions, even with a clear invitation, would never have pursued her after she made it plain that his advances were unwelcome.

"I haven't anything to fear," said Louisa-Margaretta, though her cheeks looked rather pink as she said it. "Judith, you know my character by now. I am without fear."

"Yes, very nearly," said Judith, wondering at her friend. "But you do sometimes fear for those who are close to you. Your brothers, for example. Your parents."

Louisa-Margaretta had been looking at Judith, but she turned her head sharply to peer into the lighted windows of the rectory. "I suppose they cannot help sharing a name with me, so yes, I do fear for them at times," she said. "But everyone else on earth should have the wisdom to avoid me."

Judith drew a breath. She knew she was about to hear of the reason that her friend had been out of spirits, and that her instincts had been correct. It was not only to do with the certain knowledge that Mr Rodrigo, whom Louisa-Margaretta still adored, was about to be married. Nor, Judith was sure, was it solely fear of Mr Fortescue's malicious intentions regarding the Haddington family. Something else troubled her friend. And Louisa-Margaretta, who always said too much rather than too little, had refrained from sharing it even with Judith.

"Louisa-Margaretta," said Judith. "It is an honour to be your friend. Nobody ought to be avoiding you."

Louisa-Margaretta's voice was dry and hard. "Speaking of friends, here comes your Mr Barnwell and the rector."

"My Mr Barnwell?" asked Judith hastily, but they had no time to speak again before they met the young curate. He had not come out in his coat. Rather, he seemed quite ready to entertain both ladies indoors.

"I am quite sorry I cannot join you," said Louisa-Margaretta. "I only came to invite Mr St Clair to dine with us tonight and to insist that he bring his daughters."

"Indeed, I had heard about your visitor," said Mr Barnwell. "I am sure it will be a pleasure to meet everyone on Sunday."

"Oh, Madame Chatel will not be in church," said Louisa-Margaretta. "She is a Catholic and very devout in her own way. And the Duke almost never bothers to come to church of a Sunday, or so I have heard."

Mr Barnwell blinked. "Mrs Haddington is so very pious. I had not thought—"

Louisa-Margaretta laughed. "So very demanding, you mean? Yes, that is fair to say of my mother. I suppose if anyone can get a lazy rich man into a pew, it is she, although she certainly can't force him to benefit from it."

Mr Barnwell cleared his throat. "We all benefit, of course. And since your mother has been generous enough to supply very comfortable pews for guests and visitors, even more may benefit through her generosity."

Louisa-Margaretta laughed again, and Judith could see that it was quite genuine. Though her friend was deeply concerned about something, it still did not entirely take the fun out of making sport of her mother's religiosity.

"Mama would have everyone stand, in fact. The very old

would be allowed to go to the wall and sit, as Mama has nothing but the deepest love for ancient souls, but she would have the rest of us standing to show our devotion. But most of our guests wanted a private pew, so she compromised on one with low walls. That way, we might not be separate from our brothers and sisters while we listen to Mr St Clair."

Mr Barnwell tilted his head. "Many of our patrons feel that contemplating a clergyman's words in private silence is more edifying than worrying about a neighbor who might be inattentive or sick."

Louisa-Margaretta grinned. "It is all very well for you to jump to the defense of your fellow clergyman, Mr Barnwell, and I suppose you are defending the patrons who would not like to be bothered by their fellow man. But you needn't trouble yourself. Mama is the first person to criticise gossip, yet she is somehow also the first who wishes to know what might be happening with her fellow creatures. In London, there is plenty of that, but she was born to live in a village, really."

She sounded rather less jubilant as she made that last statement, and Judith, though she wished to get out of the cold, had to ask her friend's meaning.

"And you were not, perhaps? Is that what you mean?"

"I cannot think that any part of me was meant to live in a village," said Louisa-Margaretta, turning serious again, almost as if Mr Barnwell were not there. It was against the rules of social discourse to share any intimate thought with a young man, particularly one of a different social standing, but she'd never held those rules in any regard.

"Where would you live?" asked Judith.

Though she herself had often thought about where she might like to move, never settling on an answer, it had not occurred to her to ask her friend the same question. She and Louisa-Margaretta, it seemed, were always moving based on rather urgent circumstances. Neither of them had the luxury of considering personal whims in those decisions.

"I would live in a city," said Louisa-Margaretta firmly.

"London?" asked Mr. Barnwell.

"No, life is very dull in town. A foreign city, where I knew nobody. And I would spend each day exploring."

Judith smiled, but she was gentle when she spoke to her friend. "I must confess I can hardly imagine you in a place where you could neither ride nor hunt."

"Oh, I would have a country house and do all of my hunting there," said Louisa-Margaretta. She had no trace of shame in her voice. Plainly, she thought a country house to be a very ordinary thing and saw living in at least two places as an exceedingly normal situation. Judith glanced quickly at Mr Barnwell and saw that he also smiled in amusement. He met her eyes for a moment then cleared his throat.

"Miss St Clair—"

"Welcome, Miss Haddington, Judith," said Judith's father, who was walking out to them slowly.

"You'll be cold," said Judith hastily. "Papa, we had better go in."

"I won't keep you out of doors," said Louisa-Margaretta. "But Mama asked me to invite you and both your daughters to dine with us tonight. Judith tells me you have no prior engagement and that we may look forward to the pleasure of your company. And the invitation includes you, Mr Barnwell, of course."

She walked away before Judith's father, who had begun to cough, could object.

"Mr St Clair," said Mr Barnwell. "We heard from Miss Haddington that the Duke's attendance at religious services has been somewhat limited in the past. Perhaps we might—"

"The cold," said Judith, unable to speak as forcefully as she wished but grimacing as she took her father's arm before leading him outside.

"I will not perish from cold, Judith," he said, his voice gentle. "But I do wish your friend would have given us leave not to attend the meal. If I attend, I must make excuses for you and Miriam."

They did not speak again until they had entered the house. Judith, happy to be out of her coat, went to the fire in their sitting room. Her father and Mr Barnwell followed her there.

"Come get warm, Papa," she said. "Sit closer to the fire."

"Perhaps we could convince the Duke, sir," said Mr Barnwell, also addressing Judith's father.

Judith sighed, trying not to glare at Mr Barnwell, who seemed to regard any mention of the rector's health as mere inconvenient interruption to their true work of bringing more souls to their church.

"It is only a little supper, Papa," she said. "And I am sure Mrs Haddington and the Duke will take it amiss if we do not attend."

"Yes," said her father. "But I do wonder..."

He did not finish his thought, and Mr Barnwell was only too happy to interrupt. Judith left the two of them there, speaking about pews and visitors, and went to tell her sister of the invitation and begin preparations for the dinner.

If Louisa-Margaretta's usual machinations had any effect, Judith might be sitting near Morgan, and she hardly knew how she would bear it. It would be the first meal they had shared in a great many months, and she would have to pretend to be a rather indifferent acquaintance. The ruse would require her not to mention the steady love that had sustained her through dark times. It was something Judith ought to dread, yet she found herself counting the minutes until they could set out, her secret held to her like a warm but dangerous flame.

15

Louisa-Margaretta was seated next to the painter's daughter at dinner. Mademoiselle Chatel did not appear inclined to converse with anyone, and even Louisa-Margaretta's efforts at persuading her into a conversation went nearly unnoticed at first. Which was unfortunate, as Louisa-Margaretta was quickly running through the few words and grammatical structures that she had retained from her extensive lessons in French. The things she did remember seemed to come primarily from songs, not from the many hours she had spent slumped over lessons.

"What food do you like, Mademoiselle?" she asked, her patience beginning to wane. If they came to a point where she could not think of any more questions, she would be forced to sit in silence like an imbecile or recite a series of dull statements.

But with that question, at last, the young lady came to life. "I love all foods," she said, and she went on a great deal about French delicacies that Louisa-Margaretta did not recognise. Mademoiselle Chatel talked about her anticipation of Michaelmas, speaking of the roast goose as a very special delicacy.

Louisa-Margaretta hated goose and ate only a few bites each year because her mother strongly insisted. "With the great many people who cannot afford ever to eat this meat," Mama would begin, and Louisa-Margaretta, shrugging, would chew on tiny morsels of meat while wrinkling her nose. Indeed, the only time Louisa-Margaretta ever ate like a proper lady was when she truly detested the dish before her but was prodded into eating a very little bit. It was amusing to hear the young Frenchwoman speak of goose as something rather special.

"I hope the goose is, well, it is, erm, good goose," said Louisa-Margaretta, sighing at the end of her sentence. She had been meaning to tell the guest in French that she hoped very much that the goose would please her, but she could hardly manage even a simple phrase. Mademoiselle Chatel, for the first time, looked genuinely happy rather than sour and quiet. Louisa-Margaretta did not regret paying little attention during her French lessons, but she did wonder if she ought to get Judith to spend some time with the young woman. As lonely as Louisa-Margaretta felt in Wycliff Castle, at least she had a means of communicating with other young people. Without that, she felt sure that she would go mad.

Madame Chatel, on the other hand, seemed to be managing quite nicely in English. She glared at Louisa-Margaretta's cousin, Mr Morgan Ramsbury, with a queer expression in her eyes.

"I would do anything rather than have my country fall into the hands of murdering imbeciles again," she said. "I suppose you are one of those fashionable young men who think that the pretty language of the interlopers is a good reason for bloodshed?"

Louisa-Margaretta suppressed a snort. Her cousin was hardly a fashionable man, and she could not imagine him having anything to do with bloodshed. Mr St Clair, who also took a very dim view of fighting and war, had made some excuse and refused to attend. According to what little Judith had been able to whisper to Louisa-Margaretta, her father did not wish Miriam to go, so Judith had attended alone with the promise that she would spend the entire visit in Louisa-Margaretta's company. Perhaps the rector was not quite as silly as she had thought. He must have sensed something improper between his daughter and Cousin Morgan. Otherwise, why would he have insisted on that?

The result was rather sad for Cousin Morgan. Not only would he surely be unable to steal even a minute with his pretty little fiancée, but he was also to be alone at the table with his strange views, and Louisa-Margaretta could not help finding him rather pitiful. Indeed, even the painter's words had already put a pained expression on his face.

"I think there is never any excuse for cruelty, Madame."

"Cruelty! Being killed for going to a little birthday party —would you say that is not cruel? No, you have no idea how it was in France and should count yourself lucky."

Cousin Morgan picked up his fork. Poor man! Louisa-Margaretta had to smile. Her cousin might not be a murderer, but he was surely an imbecile if he had expected Madame Chatel, who had painted Marie Antoinette's portrait more than once, to have any revolutionary sympathies.

"I am sorry that I have offended you, Madame," he said, timid even in his groveling, poor man.

The painter sniffed. "Do not be sorry for offending me.

Be sorry for holding sentiments that are so wildly wrong they have desecrated entire nations. I will endeavour to think of you as merely stupid rather than malicious."

Louisa-Margaretta was even more amused when she saw Judith turn pink and quickly glance at Cousin Morgan before taking on Madame Chatel.

"He is neither, Madame."

The entire table had snapped to attention, the battle of wits as entertaining as any duel.

"Miss St Clair," said Madame Chatel, "I am sorry. This is not talk fit for a church."

People were always making such comments to Judith, thought Louisa-Margaretta, and it only proved how little they understood her. Judith always claimed that God was present in the everyday and especially in the exchange of ideas. She did not shy away from philosophy, and rather than avoiding contrarian viewpoints, she seemed to seek them out. It was one reason she had ended up with Cousin Morgan, whose relentless questioning of the Church of England had brought him to a very strange spiritual conclusion. Louisa-Margaretta did not think the Quakers knew any more about God than clergymen like Judith's father, though she was impressed by the way they treated all people as equals. She found their philosophy rather inconvenient when directed toward others, but she would always remember how well the Quakers had insisted on treating her, even when she'd insisted on being perfectly horrid.

"It is as well we are not in church, then," answered Judith in French. Louisa-Margaretta was very pleased to be able to understand from the context. And she was even more thrilled when she noticed that she could understand Madame Chatel. The artist had decided to speak in sentences that were clear and slow as if she thought Judith lacking in comprehension.

"As you are a rector's daughter in a provincial English village, it does not surprise me that you do not have an informed opinion," said Madame Chatel. "This gentleman, Mr Ramsbury, has traveled widely, and so he must pretend to know more than he does."

"I can form an opinion based on my own experience," mumbled Judith, but she did not make more of an answer. Apparently, in trying to defend her beloved, she had lost her way.

"Indeed," said Mama, "we are all of different minds because we have lived different lives. How could it be otherwise?"

"In all our lives, we have seen poverty, if not in our own circumstances then in the trials suffered by others," said Cousin Morgan in English. He looked pointedly at Mrs Haddington. "Is it any wonder, when so many are hungry, that many should eventually be persuaded that there is no dignity in a system that gives a man a palace or a poorhouse based on no more than his birth?"

Louisa-Margaretta saw Judith, still red, hiding a ghost of a smile. Mama firmly believed that every person was deserving of dignity and often used "palace or poorhouse" when she attempted to convince others to join her on her many visits to the poorest of their neighbours in the village. But that did not mean that she would feel she did not deserve the wealth and position that was her birthright.

"And yet," said Mama with a frown, "does it follow that we should force everyone into the same poverty or only that those in the palaces ought to do their duty toward their fellow man?"

Louisa-Margaretta smiled wickedly, giving her cousin a

wink that he pretended not to see. "Yes, Cousin Morgan, we should force our wonderful Prinny to do his duty. Is he not proof that our system of government is eminently functional? We have a man born to a palace who neglects the poor, along with all his other duties, but never fear, he must surely be an exception."

Mama's face grew tense. She might share generously when it was time to give alms, but having been raised with the idea that her family deserved to be waited upon in generous quarters, she would never agree with the radical political sentiments that some in the younger generation espoused freely.

"His father, had he been able to continue, would have seen to all of his duties without shirking once." Mama shook her head. "And so do most men of property and most men of the family. I am sure that our kind ruler will grow into his role, as do so many children."

That was said with a pointed look at Louisa-Margaretta, who nearly jumped when the Duke began to speak. She had completely forgotten that the man taking ungentlemanly large spoonfuls of soup was a relative of the Prince Regent, as he had not taken the slightest interest in the conversation. He had been sitting in a most ill-mannered fashion, talking with Mr Galpin for the entire duration of their meal. It was strange, Louisa-Margaretta reflected, that the order of precedence at the table seemed to have changed, as at their first meal, Mama had not put Mr Galpin and the Duke together. Perhaps the Duke had asked to be next to his friend and his hostess had accommodated him. Indeed, Mama had already made more than one comment about how the Duke was so used to having exactly what he wished for at every moment, it was exceedingly difficult to anticipate his every need in such a remote setting.

"Such dull things, so many of these duties," said the Duke. "And every year the same! All of these ladies presented at court, the same dresses, the same tedious parade. That's why men ought to seek out rather more interesting company, what?"

He clapped a hand on Mr Galpin's arm, grinning lecherously at the only men present at the table, Louisa-Margaretta's cousin and father. Cousin Morgan pursed his lips. Papa turned red as if deeply ashamed, and Louisa-Margaretta could see him shifting in his seat, which he did only when he felt very uncomfortable. Usually, even her taciturn papa could manage a simple rejoinder, but he said nothing, and Mama looked temporarily unable to rescue him.

Fortunately for them all, Madame Chatel had turned to the man with a fire blazing in her eyes.

"So men who are tasked with taking care of an entire country can be released from their duties if they do not find them amusing, eh? That is an interesting way of going about things, to be sure. Why, when I was in Paris—"

"You saw many men like me, those who took their duties of pleasure and entertainment quite seriously," said the Duke. "Why else would the people rise? But unlike my family, I feel no such threat is very likely here. We have already lost some of our colonies, and that will be that. If they want to live in horrid little cities such as that place they call New York, let them, poor fools. It is better to live in York itself. Surely, any fool could see that."

Louisa-Margaretta, who had hitherto been most relieved that the Duke had not found anything she said offensive, drew in a breath. "I am not sure that we ought to call those of us who seek a new home fools."

"We should not speak lightly of the bloodshed either," said Madame Chatel, who was not exactly agreeing with

Louisa-Margaretta but certainly displeased with the Duke. "Real lives have been lost and all in service of the vanity of a bunch of silly men in Philadelphia. I wept when I saw news of those battles, and now they have the gall to pretend to be an independent nation! God save us."

"God has very little to do with it," said Cousin Morgan, finding his voice again. He was so pious, of course he would not allow God to be a part of any battle.

"In that, we can agree," said Madame Chatel, her voice cutting. "Wishing that people should be killed or lose their homes is ungodly."

"You have a new home here," said the Duke, belching. "We all have a comfortable home and most excellent food, away from those thieves in London. I thought we should simply catch the thief and hang him, but being here with all these beautiful and refined ladies is just as pleasant as finally having a worthy portrait."

Even Mama looked ashamed at the man's ill breeding, but as hostess, she only gave an empty smile.

"I hope you all will enjoy our next course. I confess, our kitchen garden is a wonder of Derbyshire. I would have expected next to nothing from such a climate, and yet we have such a yield that all our meals are sumptuous."

Madame Chatel looked as if she were on the verge of refusing the peaceful overture. She gave the Duke, who had given his attention to the next course, a poisonous look before allowing her features to settle into a false smile. Louisa-Margaretta looked about to see if anyone else had noticed, but she saw only that everyone was eager to sample the meat, if only to save themselves from such an unpleasant conversation.

The rest of the meal passed in relative peace, and shortly after, Judith made her apologies. Louisa-Margaretta was prevented from speaking to her by her mama's insistence that she sing. She thought that might have been another ruse of Mama's to prevent arguments, but if so, Louisa-Margaretta did not greatly mind. She might not have the sort of political background or discipline that would impress Madame Chatel, but Louisa-Margaretta knew the woman's voice to be quite lovely.

16

———

Judith had to remind herself why she bothered riding with her friend. It always involved dragging herself over to Wycliff Castle while wearing one of Louisa-Margaretta's old riding habits. No matter how many times Judith tried to alter hers, she could never get it to fit properly. It always looked like it was made for a larger, handsomer woman with light colouring. Which, of course, it had been.

That morning was no different, and after Judith struggled with the dress for a bit, she went over to Miriam to beg her sister's assistance. In other times, Judith might have been too proud, but Miriam had more of an eye for fashion and might be swifter with her stitches.

She smiled, standing before the mirror and holding the dress up in front of her sister. "Judith, it's no good trying to look like the beautiful Miss Haddington. You should get a riding habit in a colour that suits you better. Brown, perhaps, or a very deep grey."

Judith snatched her clothing back, turning away from the mirror. "Thank you, Miriam. I'm not sure where the money would come from, but I am most grateful for your opinion."

Miriam sighed, still gazing into the mirror, and fixed a curl that had come loose. "I suppose we cannot all afford to live in castles. That is true. Though I'm sure that entertaining Dukes would be lovely. Papa wanted to keep me from going to the meal last night. Did you hear him? If I had not promised Caroline specially, I would have gone. To think that her birthday kept me away from such a meal!"

"They will be eager to invite you again," said Judith. "But I am not sure I would have you go either."

She felt a prickling of unease. Miriam did not look as young as she had when they had first arrived in their new home. As she grew older, her bloom was ever lovelier, and she was one of the beauties of the neighbourhood. Her features, being somewhat soft, would never be as striking as Louisa-Margaretta's, but she was very pretty. And she dressed in carefully chosen colours that she might show her fine blue eyes and beautiful dark hair to advantage.

Judith often felt that her muddy eyes and her tawny hair were much the same colour and that she looked dull as a result. For some time, she had stopped thinking of her looks. When she was much younger, she did not think of her own beauty because she felt that she was very plain. Later, she felt herself drawn to the religious practice of "Dressing Plain" as she had learned more about the Quakers and their beliefs. And more recently, she had cared a great deal what Mr Morgan Ramsbury thought, without paying any attention to whether other men or women took notice of her.

But gazing at her sister, she was reminded that she had always known Miriam was the more beautiful St Clair. She did not resent that any longer. It was such a natural fact that it wanted little scrutiny. There was a great deal of their father's features in Miriam's face, but youth and femininity made them beautiful, and Miriam had their mother's smile. Judith could see a bit of her mother in her own brow, but mostly, she felt that she did not share the sort of beauty that both her mother and Miriam could take as a given.

Judith's plainness, however she chose to describe it, had not protected her from the Duke. And if he were presented with another St Clair sister, one who was younger and prettier, how was he going to behave? All morning, Judith had been dreading her ride but was thankful for the fact that it would not involve going inside Wycliff Castle. She was so nearly one of the family that she could go straight to the stables without giving offense, and the lads who worked in the stables would not think it strange if she asked them to take a message to Louisa-Margaretta. The thought of seeing the Duke sit and laugh at his own jokes, as she had the day before, made her feel immediately ill. Judith typically ate little, but the night before, she had finished several of the courses, eating more than was proper for a lady, as she did not want her pale face and sickly demeanor to draw any scrutiny.

No, she could not invite Miriam.

Judith cleared her throat. "I have the general impression we are not to spend time with the Duke or Madame Chatel," she said. "Louisa-Margaretta has arranged for us to ride with Mademoiselle Marie Chatel, the painter's daughter, and the Duchess."

Miriam wrinkled her nose then picked up an ornament and put it in her hair, checking the mirror closely to see the effect. "Oh, all right. I suppose I shall go to the Chandlers' after all. Sally said that both of them are dull creatures."

Judith sighed. She should have reprimanded Miriam for

gossiping, and perhaps even spoken to Sally, their maid. But she had long ago discovered that the village, though it certainly had its charms, was a place where information flowed as freely as a river in springtime. Louisa-Margaretta was correct. Each inhabitant, whether she considered herself a disinterested observer or an incorrigible gossip, spread the same general set of facts about others. If Judith attempted to interfere with the news from Wycliff Castle concerning the exotic new visitors, she would succeed only in driving the conversations away from her own hearing.

"I hope you have a pleasant morning there," Judith said, staring down at her garment and willing herself to wear it. She hated having to face the stable master of Wycliff Castle all on her own, and if she arrived early or at the appointed hour, the sour old man would act as if he were shocked that he should be forced to procure a mount for such a poor horsewoman.

"It should be pleasant enough," Miriam said. "But truly, Judith, things are not well with the Chandler family. Has Mr Barnwell had no success with the Haddingtons and his scheme to get their assistance in selling some of the paintings? Perhaps he is not a man of his word."

"He is," Judith insisted, wondering briefly why she defended the young curate so quickly. "But I am not sure it is easy to get an audience at the moment. Perhaps when Mrs Haddington is less occupied with her visitors, she will be able to spare a moment for a young artist."

"It is in this very moment that he ought to press for such a thing," said Miriam. "For after the famous painter leaves, how is she going to help an unknown artist like one of the Chandlers?"

After a rather long pause, Judith sighed, pressing against the door. "Very well, Miriam. I know what you ask of me."

"You could hardly do less," said her sister, her look reproachful. "Only, look how rich the Haddingtons are, and Madame Chatel as well, I am sure. And the Chandlers are so poor."

"Yes," said Judith. "I will ask, that is. I can promise no more."

"You need not promise anything at all," said Miriam. "Simply find a buyer who likes one painting or perhaps two, and the whole family will eat goose for Michaelmas."

Judith looked down. Having spent a great many years with no money to spare, before finally enjoying the small bounty of her own savings and her father's new position, Judith disliked speaking about money almost as much as Louisa-Margaretta did. While Louisa-Margaretta found the subject dull, to Judith, it was very painful.

"I'll see what she can manage" was all she said in response to her sister.

17

———

"You ought to be riding sidesaddle," said a scandalised Duchess to Louisa-Margaretta. "Women are not allowed to sit this way."

Louisa-Margaretta did not answer. Indeed, she usually did sit like a lady, though she had confessed to Judith that she often sat with one leg on either side like a man, without using a saddle, if she could be certain that she would not be observed. The stable master, though he did not approve, would bring her a horse without a saddle if she asked.

"The winters here are so horrid," she had told Judith. "None of these riding habits will ever keep one warm. A horse's back is better than anything else."

Judith rode only sidesaddle, as most women did, but she did it poorly. She saw that the Duchess had a practised air, but she had none of the natural grace of Louisa-Margaretta. Mademoiselle Chatel was having some difficulty controlling her horse, but she had an enthusiasm that matched Louisa-Margaretta's. As her mare tried to eat one of the few remaining stalks of grass, she laughed as she reined the horse in.

"Thank you for the escape," she said. "I thought one more day confined to that room would make me go mad."

Judith nearly coughed, and the Duchess glared at the other young woman.

"A proper lady does not ever find her lot dull or go mad, for that matter," she said.

Judith did not even attempt to correct such thinking. She had learned some time ago that most people regarded madness as the worst possible fate, worse even than death. The view that she had learned from Morgan and his religious companions, that people who were mad deserved to have warm meals and civilised conversation, was not the prevailing one.

Louisa-Margaretta did not bother to hold her tongue. "Many ladies go mad," she said. "In fact, the conditions of a grand lady's life are perfect for madness, in many ways."

Judith cleared her throat. "We should follow the path. But this ride needs to be a short one, or we may tire the horses."

Mademoiselle Chatel gave a nod to Louisa-Margaretta. "Thank you. I do believe that I felt more freedom in my mind in a tiny Paris apartment than I have in any of these grand houses, but whenever I tell my mother, she simply chastises me to occupy myself."

The Duchess looked as if she approved, but Louisa-Margaretta was going on.

"A grand lady is confined to a home, or a room in some cases, unable to move freely about. Barred from discussing subjects of interest in company, not permitted to learn more about them. If my family were poor, I should have to go out and earn a wage, and things would be much easier."

"Oh, come now," burst out Judith. "I am not sure we

ought to call boiling dirty cloth in winter an easy occupation. Or burning one's hands in hot ovens."

"I'll argue about the ovens," said Mademoiselle Chatel cheerfully, though it sounded as if she meant to praise them rather than argue about them. "It is difficult to get them heated properly, and here, it is so cold! Mademoiselle, your cook must be very brilliant indeed."

"She has food at the ready for me, without reporting me to my mother in every instance," said Louisa-Margaretta. "Even when I go riding without anything planned in advance, there is always plenty for me to take out. That, to me, is all that is required of a cook."

Mademoiselle Chatel nodded along. "Of course! Whenever I eat during the morning, my mother calls it a waste. She says one ought to not take too much refreshment before the first sitting. But she is the painter, the one with sittings. I need only assist her, and it is ever so much more tedious when my stomach is empty."

Judith still looked rather skeptical. "You like to cook yourself, then, Mademoiselle?"

She had been expecting a negative answer, but the young woman only smiled. "More than anything! And I am a rather good cook, though I ought not to boast of such a thing."

"Certainly not," said the Duchess. "Women of quality are expected to supervise the work that happens in the kitchen of their homes, not to do the cooking. The more ignorance, the greater the elegance of a lady."

She sounded as if she were repeating a maxim from a book, and Judith could sense, rather than hear, Louisa-Margaretta sighing and urging her horse to go faster.

"That is exactly it," said Mademoiselle Chatel firmly, not

at all offended. "When I was a child, I used to cook constantly. There was only one hired girl to help us, so my mother and I both had to do nearly everything. And she hates cooking, so I was always in the little kitchen. But once she earned more from her paintings, and especially when we began to live apart from my father, she started to insist that I should act like a lady and forget it all."

The Duchess gave a nod of approval, but Judith only frowned. "Have you forgotten, then?"

"No, of course not! But I cannot steal enough moments here to cook, even if I were permitted. My mother is being unusually horrid and insisting on keeping me with her always."

Judith looked carefully at the two women with them. But the Duchess had gently urged her horse along, and Louisa-Margaretta was quite a bit ahead, so Judith could not tell what they were thinking.

"Do you know why your mother is strict with you, Mademoiselle Chatel?" she asked.

"I have not the faintest notion," said the young lady, bumping along gracelessly on her horse. "She keeps saying the painting will be stolen, but I have no idea how she could be so sure."

Unless she means to steal it herself, though Judith immediately. She would be surprised if Madame Chatel had stolen all of the paintings, but her cavalier insistence that the painting would soon be gone had made Judith wonder whether she might, perhaps, be the thief.

After their first polite conversation, none of the ladies made a great effort to converse, and so the rest of the ride passed before they could speak. But Judith found herself looking carefully into the woods, even checking the windows of Wycliff Castle. If there was one thief, he might have come down from London. Or he might have painters do the thieving for him. In which case, it was very unlikely that he would ever be discovered.

18

––––––––––

Louisa-Margaretta hesitated at the door of her mother's favourite room. The State Music Room was less practical than the simpler Music Room, though it did contain more than one instrument. The decorations were more ornate, more fit for the sort of company that they never seemed to have. Though with the Duke visiting, they had already used the room more than once. Perhaps Mama was proud.

On a more usual day, Louisa-Margaretta would have gone straight into the room to inform Mama of their plan. But it had gotten more difficult to speak with her mother during the visit. Everything centred around pleasing the Duke and his retinue, and Louisa-Margaretta was already tired of spending so many hours on such a dull man.

She sighed, deciding that she must go in after all. Her mother had a writing desk in the room, and she liked to sit near the window and write her letters there each day, reveling in the elegance of the arrangements and the quiet location of the room itself. Mama took delight in keeping up with her correspondence, but she also wrote her letters quickly. Anything sent to her would be answered not hastily but in very good time. Unlike Judith, however, she did not sit frowning over her pen and wondering at the words she put on each page, even going so far as to waste ink and paper writing some parts all over again.

Louisa-Margaretta did not respond to half her own letters, finding even her mother's habit of sitting down to write letters each morning unbearably tedious. She hesitated at the door for one more moment, still unwilling to go in and speak to her mother.

She was soon glad that she had not entered, because it appeared that her mother had company.

"I am, indeed, very sorry for you," said Madame Chatel. "My daughter and I have had our troubles, but she goes where I do. Thank goodness, I have not had the misfortune of resettling only for her, though I do think we would have stayed in France longer if I had not been worried for her safety."

She was speaking English well, Louisa-Margaretta noted, quite sure that Madame Chatel usually spoke French more due to her lack of interest in the company than any lack of facility with the English language.

"You do not need to feel sorry for us," said Mama, though Louisa-Margaretta thought she heard a hint of anger in her mother's tone. "We are happy to have found a new home here. Indeed, I am happier here than I ever was anywhere else, and it is convenient for my husband's business matters."

The latter part was true, Louisa-Margaretta knew. With her father travelling frequently to Manchester, a home in Derbyshire was very convenient. But she wondered if Mama was truly at her happiest. She certainly seemed to love their new home and the village, and she had gotten her wish in keeping Louisa-Margaretta well away from Isaac Rodrigo, but she saw very little of her sons and grandchildren.

She heard the rattle of the painter's teacup. It seemed that the woman, who was so very fond of ordinary fare, did not mind being served the finest tea in the most expensive china cups.

"It is difficult with daughters," she said. "With a son, you could send him off into some profession, and as long as you had him in the right sort of place, he would improve. This is a harder thing to accomplish with a young lady."

"We did make an attempt," said Mama. "Or rather, Louisa-Margaretta herself wished to, well, to work. But the circumstances were rather unusual, and it all turned out badly, I am sorry to say. Though I blame those who ought to have taken more care."

Mama blames Judith, thought Louisa-Margaretta, though for some reason, she was careful enough not to say so directly to Madame Chatel. It was really rather amusing that her mother considered Judith a sort of aunt or chaperone. Truly, Judith had not been at fault, though after their adventures the previous summer, they had both returned with regrets. As always, Louisa-Margaretta had acted exactly as she wished, and now she had only to repent. The sword of Damocles was over Judith's head, not just the heads of the Haddingtons, and if Mama knew that Louisa-Margaretta had caused it all, she might have treated poor Judith with a bit more sympathy.

"It is a shame your daughter has no talent for painting," said Madame Chatel. "How I would love to help another young woman with gifts in this regard! It was so difficult for me to enter the Royal Academy, although now it hardly matters. But alas, my dear Marie also has no eye. She seems content enough to follow me about, poor thing."

"Your daughter has other gifts, I am sure," said Mama.

"That ought to be true," said Madame Chatel. "We cannot allow any young woman to waste her gifts, though, can we? For if she ends up married to a scoundrel, as I was, an independent living will be of more use to her than any settlement."

Mama cleared her throat. "Louisa-Margaretta need not worry about such a thing. Her brothers are all devoted to her. She would have a home with any of them."

Louisa-Margaretta stifled a laugh. Though she believed that all of her brothers loved her, in their way, she would feel at home only with Percival. By rights, if her father were gone, she should live at Wycliff Castle with Augustus, since he was to inherit. But she could hardly imagine living with him and his punctilious wife, and unless he retired from the diplomatic service, he was hardly going to be eager to live in Derbyshire.

"I confess, Madame," said Madame Chatel, warming to her subject, "I am most concerned for Mademoiselle Louisa-Margaretta. If she were my daughter—"

"I am sure I am not your daughter," said Louisa-Margaretta, walking into the room. "I resemble my mother much too closely, as you yourself have noted."

"Dearest," said Mama, going to Louisa-Margaretta and embracing her.

Louisa-Margaretta stepped back from her mother. "I wanted to tell both of you that Mademoiselle Chatel, the Duchess, Miss St Clair, and I have made plans to ride tomorrow. We are to take a picnic. I hope you will be able to do without us."

"I am not certain," began Madame Chatel, but Mama was firm.

"Certainly we can, dearest."

"Excellent," said Louisa-Margaretta. "For the moment, since I see you have no need of me, I am going to go out and sketch."

19

Louisa-Margaretta had not done a bit of sketching. She could not even bring herself to take anything out of the satchel. Instead, she stared at the lake, pulling leaves off the thorny bush next to her and throwing them down the hillside. Some of the thorns were so long and sharp that they pricked her even through her gloves, but she did not care. Her body sought destruction.

When her parents had removed her to Wycliff Castle, she had been angry. She had fancied herself an imprisoned princess, and at every moment, she had petulantly tried to fight her mother and father. Mama, because she was more often home and could tolerate her daughter's displeasure, bore the brunt of it. Louisa-Margaretta was angry with her father, but his business often took him away, and if she scolded him, he might come near to weeping and apologize for not having done better by her. It was very tedious. Mama, who was stronger, was a better target for her daughter's anger.

But all that time, Louisa-Margaretta had been sure of one thing. Her parents did not want her throwing away her future. Louisa-Margaretta felt certain that they believed that she possessed the promise of a bright and beautiful life. They expected her not only to marry well but also to become an accomplished lady of purpose like her mother, an example to any community she visited. Her parents had always told her that she was clever and that though she must be guarded in terms of her reputation, she might still accomplish great things. In fact, one of the reasons Mama had continuously forced Louisa-Margaretta into the company of the Countess was because she wanted her daughter to see the role a wife might play in diplomacy. If the Countess had always seemed a strange, nervy sort of woman, apt to become upset about a threadbare cushion and rather ignorant of the affairs of other countries, well, that was not Mama's intention.

But Louisa-Margaretta now realized that she had been absolutely mistaken in her perception of her parents. Instead of wishing that she might grace society with her gifts, they must have been preparing for her to fail. Her mother had been trying to protect her, but neither of her parents expected her to amount to anything. They did not even think her fit to be the wife of someone without a place in society. It was as if, after everything with Isaac, she had done even more to convince them that she ought to be neither valued nor trusted.

Perhaps it was as well that she and Isaac had already had their time together, then. She was giddy when she thought back on their conversations, on the few kisses they had managed to steal when they were unobserved. How differently she had felt about everything then! Both she and Isaac had been eager for the engagement so that they might end up married eventually. To Louisa-Margaretta, marriage sounded like good fun. She could be alone with her beloved, in a home of their choosing, with societal sanction! They could do whatever they liked, and nobody would find it scandalous, only natural. It was equal parts joke and blessing.

But those days, when she had imagined things would improve for her, were all that remained to Louisa-Margaretta. Her Isaac was already living out that vision with some other woman an ocean away, and she was to stay in Wycliff Castle alone until one of her brothers took pity on her. She would be damned if she would marry now, as it was clear that her parents thought so little of her that they did not even expect such a thing.

And just as Louisa-Margaretta was silently making one of her many vows of spinsterhood, that time predicated not on the faithfulness of her beloved—Oh, Isaac! How she wished he had been a different sort of man!—but on the hopelessness of her situation, a man came striding up the hill.

"What troubles you, Miss Haddington?" His tired eyes gleamed. "If you fall to weeping over this scene straightaway, you will never get any sketching done."

That was met with an uncharacteristic sob from Louisa-Margaretta. Mr. Chandler's ill-timed joke had only proved that nobody at all understood her feelings.

"I am sorry," he said. "It was an impertinence. Truly, Miss Haddington, please."

He felt about in his pockets, and Louisa-Margaretta was conscious of his growing impatience as he tried and failed to find something for her.

"I have only these rags stained with paint, I'm ashamed to say," he said. "Hardly a fit handkerchief. But I am sorry for my words. I have just rarely ever seen you out of spirits, Miss Haddington, if you will pardon my saying so."

And as he had before, he moved closer to her.

She could not have described her feelings. Her body was weak with the exhaustion of being a disappointment to her parents, a burden to her brothers, a laughably sad case for pity in the eyes of the famous Madame Chatel. And yet the thoughts of Isaac had made her feel an angry, energetic thrumming of a passion that she had never been able to extinguish.

She kissed Mr Chandler, and his surprise was instantly made known to her, along with his delight in what might have passed for her affection.

20

―――――

Judith could have asked anyone in the house where Louisa-Margaretta was to be found. Someone certainly could have told her, as every time any member of the household breathed, there seemed to be at least three servants nearby to take note.

But Judith was ashamed not to know what had become of her best friend. She quickly learned that Louisa-Margaretta was not with her mother and Madame Chatel. Though Judith was afraid of the stables, she could tell by observing them from the window that Louisa-Margaretta had not been there to take one of the horses out again. All of the boys had the distinct look of relief that came with being done with their duties for a time. They might still have to do a great deal of mucking out, but tugging their forelocks in front of a fine lady was not something they would have to do again. At least not immediately.

She shied away from the room where the Duke had been sitting for his portrait, seeking instead a place that was comforting to her. The airy room that had once been used as a schoolroom for some cousins was a perfect haven. It was always unused, and one of the chairs was comfortable enough. The room had no fire, so it was quite cold, but Judith was still warm from her ride. She took advantage of one of the shawls that had been placed there some time ago.

The room had a menacing presence, as the Duke's portrait was stored, uncovered, in the corner. There was a cloth that Judith had placed across the horrid thing, but as she looked more closely, she found that the Duke's likeness did not scare her. Madame Chatel had not captured his expression or his true nature but had portrayed a man who was taller and kinder, without any pockmarks in his skin. It was not as interesting as the portrait she was making of Mrs Haddington. Rather, it was so favourable as to be a sophisticated mockery. The Duke looked like a statue, not a human. Judith put the cloth down on a table instead of covering the painting.

As she sat, she allowed her features to become less composed, her gaze less certain. In front of the Duchess and the painter's taciturn daughter, she had not been able to speak freely, but the truth was that Wycliff Castle was no longer her haven. She did not wish to stay there another moment, and only the certainty that she would not be discovered let her feel at ease. She had to speak with Louisa-Margaretta. The things that Mademoiselle Chatel had insinuated could not be ignored. If someone was going to speak to Madame Chatel, it would have to happen soon, before she could go through with the theft. Louisa-Margaretta would know how to hide the painting. Even after only a few years at Wycliff Castle, she was sure to know many of the best hiding places.

21

———

Louisa-Margaretta arranged her dress carefully. It had only just occurred to her that they were in a place where they could have been discovered by nearly anyone. Though the woods had seemed deserted and her mother hated the coarse, ill-bred men who claimed to go about catching poachers, still, the estate had plenty of workers who might have passed that way. Not to mention any of the Misses Chandler, who were all so fond of sketching.

Her heart caught in her throat when she thought of them, and she stole another glance at their father. He was arranging his paints and brushes but slowly and with a knowing smile, having taken little care with his own clothing. She wondered if he was practised at that sort of betrayal. The man was married, but perhaps he had no regard for his vows. Louisa-Margaretta, who was free in every sense, felt as guilty as she would have had she and Isaac been married. His face kept appearing in her mind as she reproached herself.

And yet she certainly understood why people risked

marriages, names, reputations. It had always seemed like a bit of a strange thought to her, but Mr Fortescue had given her a taste for the forbidden. And with Mr Chandler, she had proved that fear of scandal would not stop her.

While she had been ruminating, still in shock at the suddenness of it all, Mr Chandler gave an exaggerated, sweeping glance about him. Finding that they were still alone, he kissed her again. He murmured something and touched his hat, and Louisa-Margaretta nodded as he walked on down the path.

She swallowed then grabbed her sketching things. She could hardly begin to recall the anger that had driven her out of her home and up to that strange hillside in the first place. Naturally, after what she had overheard, her pride had been wounded, but that was hardly a good reason to run for the hills and into the arms of a most unsuitable neighbor. Perhaps Mama and Madame Chatel thought her beyond redemption, a daughter lost to the whims of passion that seized her with such shocking frequency.

She had not been intending to prove them right.

22

———

Judith saw Louisa-Margaretta walking down the hill toward her home, looking pale and determined. Judith gave a great sigh. If she had gone out the door two minutes later, she surely would have missed Louisa-Margaretta. But on seeing her friend, she felt rather put out at the hours she had wasted searching various wings of the palatial home. She could have employed her time much better, and the hour she had wasted sleeping at the hard table would have to be explained when she reached the rectory.

"Where have you been wandering?" Judith asked. "I was searching for you."

For soft-spoken Judith, it was a harsh reproach, but Louisa-Margaretta looked away. Judith noticed with some surprise that her friend was shivering.

"I went out to sketch," Louisa-Margaretta said. "Mama and Madame Chatel feel that I ought to apply myself."

Her voice sounded distant as she said it, and Judith's response was sharp.

"Perhaps you can apply yourself to seeing to your guests.

I came because you wanted me to entertain them, then you ignored all of us."

Louisa-Margaretta nodded. "Well, perhaps another day."

Judith stared at her. "You disappeared for hours and you're not going to apologise?"

Louisa-Margaretta turned back and looked at the hillside then stared at her boots. "Judith, I am not at leisure," she said. "I must go into the house and rest."

Judith could not believe her friend. Louisa-Margaretta did look much more tired than usual, but Judith was sure her friend still would have energy to speak of the art theft before languishing away in her large home.

"I wanted to go to my own home and rest," said Judith crossly. "But I could not until I spoke with you, and I had no idea where you'd gone."

Louisa-Margaretta sighed. "Well, you have spoken to me now."

"I suppose I have," said Judith, deciding at once that she did not need to voice her suspicions about Madame Chatel. If the painter was a thief, let her take her own paintings. Judith need not intervene to help the Haddingtons when they would not help themselves. All at once, she felt heartily sick of the family. Louisa-Margaretta would run off without a word to her guests, even though she should have seen how tired Judith was feeling after the ride. Mrs Haddington had been rude to Judith ever since they'd returned, though Judith had done her utmost to protect Louisa-Margaretta from Mr Fortescue. Mr Haddington was kind enough, and he always seemed eager to speak to Judith, but he was so shy that they had never once had a conversation about anything more than the weather or the colour of the hillsides. And Louisa-Margaretta's brothers did not generally even bother to visit.

That last point was perhaps the weakest one. Derbyshire was a long and expensive journey away from the residences of most of the Haddington brothers, and their parents and sister looked for excuses to go to London rather than entertaining many visitors in Wycliff Castle. Judith felt that the expense of travelling was far too great, but the Haddingtons had paid all of the expenses when she went to Essex and returned. And the tithes her father received were so impressive that he was able to help Aunt Leah on her many visits, which would never have been possible in his former position.

In spite of all that, Judith was still cross with her friend.

"You ought to go take better care of your guests," she said.

Louisa-Margaretta looked as if she were disappearing into herself, wrapping her arms about her body and staring off into the distance.

"They are not my guests," she said. "I only agreed to have them here to prove a point to my mother's horrid friend."

Judith remembered what her friend had said. "If you didn't want them here, you could have told Countess Koltsova as much. There was no need to bring a great contingent of people to Derbyshire simply because you are too proud to admit that you dislike playing the gracious hostess."

"I could have done many things differently," said Louisa-Margaretta. "But what's done is done. So you ought to go home, Judith. And I would not bother coming back soon, if I were in your position."

Her friend's manner was so cold and formal that Judith looked about, wondering if they were being observed. Perhaps Louisa-Margaretta was using cutting remarks to

Judith as a way to please her mother. But Judith saw nobody, though a cloud passed over the sun, making the day even colder.

"Very well," Judith said. "I suppose I ought to go. Take care."

She said the last part without thinking. Even when she was angry with the haughty Miss Haddington, she could not help but come out with the expressions of affectionate friendship that had become so natural to her.

Louisa-Margaretta did not return the sentiment. She only laughed bitterly.

"Oh, Judith," she said. "It is rather too late for that."

23

The rectory felt warm when Judith entered. That was the one thing she liked about the walk between Wycliff Castle and her father's house, its usefulness in chilling her enough to appreciate the smaller fires at her home. On that day, she had been thinking chiefly of the very great distance between the two homes and how it must be immoral on its face for one family to own such a great deal of land while others starved. Therefore, once she entered, she felt deep gratitude to be out of the wind and safe. And there was no cause for her to go back to Wycliff Castle. Louisa-Margaretta could manage the guests on her own, without Judith's interference, and Mr Barnwell would be the one to beg their assistance in the matter of the Chandler family. Her heart did tell her that if she stopped going over to that home, it would be more difficult for her to see Mr Morgan Ramsbury, but she forced herself to accept that natural consequence. Since he apparently thought very little of her, perhaps it was better they did not meet, though she knew that eventually, she would have to give her suitor a definite answer. She was sure that avoiding a man who was staying a mere mile away would not be very likely, but she allowed herself to leave those cares at the door. For just one evening, she wanted to be a simple person in her own home, without the complications of entertaining great personages or the fear of encountering the Duke.

Alas, she was not to get her wish. As soon as she entered the sitting room, she found all of the elder members of her family assembled and a guest there with them.

"Hello, my dear," said her father. "We were wondering when you would be in to join us."

"Mr Ramsbury has been entertaining us with stories of his studies," said Miriam. "And I always thought barristers and solicitors had dull work!"

Judith did not sit down but stared at her fiancé as he attempted to greet her in a natural manner.

"I can promise that some of it is rather dull," he said, blushing. "But I thought I ought to at least share some of the more interesting bits."

"Visitors are always expected to bring stories," said her father. "But you need not feel under any obligation, Mr Ramsbury. The pleasure of your company is enough."

Judith blushed to hear her father praise her intended, as she knew that his words were sincere. Morgan had been sitting near the fire, helping Moses craft another animal for the little collection that was supposed to belong to Noah's ark. They had a ship that Aaron had fashioned, and though it did not look a great deal like anything biblical, still, it was sturdy enough.

"You ought to visit more," said Miriam meaningfully, and her father shot her a warning glance. Miriam sighed.

"I mean, I know you may not love Wycliff Castle, but it is impossible for us to go anywhere interesting. And Miss

Haddington, your cousin, hates living here. I am sure she is very thankful for your visits."

"Miriam," said their father, but Judith frowned as she took a seat next to her sister, realising that she should attempt to act naturally around Morgan so as to avoid rousing any suspicions.

"I hope you have a very pleasant stay in Derbyshire," Judith said stiffly.

Morgan, it appeared, was not determined to act indifferent. He gave her an ironic smile, and Judith hoped that none of her family would notice that it was not quite his usual expression.

"Oh," he said. "I very much hope that I shall."

24

___

Louisa-Margaretta had the ill fortune of finding the whole company together when she entered Wycliff Castle. The trouble was that most of the servants, with the exceptions of Harriet and Cook, were exceedingly loyal to her mother. They would tell her where everyone was assembled, saying it with such emphatic politeness that it was clear they were sure that young Miss Haddington intended to join the party. That left Louisa-Margaretta no recourse apart from a sick headache. When she did not want to join a particular guest, she would say that she felt unwell and rush off toward her room to die of boredom as she pretended to be an invalid.

But on that day, Louisa-Margaretta did feel truly ill, uneasy in the body that had betrayed her. In fact, she could not help feeling that her body had betrayed Isaac, though she knew that a married man an ocean away would hardly give a fig about any weakness she might display with one of their neighbours.

That was it—Mr. Chandler was a neighbour and a rather lonely one at that. She felt like a cautionary tale.

After years of wondering why both men and women were whispered to have taken up with people in their immediate circle rather than the more notable beauties outside their orbit, she finally understood. If Louisa-Margaretta had thought of going against her better judgement by seeking a gentleman, she would not have been able to do it. She had acted chiefly upon the strength of feelings arising in the moment, with neither time nor inconvenience to stand in her way. The difficulty of making arrangements to meet in secret had probably guarded the virtue of all sorts of ladies and gentlemen. But Mr Chandler had been right before her when her heart was shaky, and now she could never change her decision. If any gossips got hold of her story, Louisa-Margaretta reflected bitterly, they would say that her scandal was especially rich given that she encountered so few gentlemen.

Those were Louisa-Margaretta's thoughts as she entered the room where the whole company had gathered, with even Madame Chatel looking rather at ease as they all had tea together. Louisa-Margaretta's mother gave her a cup, and Louisa-Margaretta stirred in a great deal of sugar. It was supposed to be good for invalids and those experiencing a great shock. Louisa-Margaretta felt as if she would never speak properly again, and the whole room had taken on shades of unreality. She thought that everyone near her must be able to read her decisions in her expression, in the shivering that she tried to calm by sitting near the fire.

"You are looking well, Miss Haddington," said the Duke as she gripped her teacup firmly, willing her fingers to stop trembling. He looked pink and flushed, as if he had been drinking wine even at that hour, and she thought she detected a hint of it on his breath as he leaned nearer.

Louisa-Margaretta took a sip of her tea without responding, so he took it upon himself to go on.

"I love it when young ladies are fond of walking," he said. "It puts the roses in their cheeks."

"I do not walk for your amusement, sir."

In another woman, it might have been said in jest. Indeed, only recently, Louisa-Margaretta herself would have said such a thing in order to flirt with a man. But that time, she was not laughing. Mademoiselle Chatel, who had been gazing into a corner, turned her attention to the arguing pair, and Mama immediately stepped in as the calm hostess.

"There are many lovely walks here, though at first I thought that Derbyshire would be a bit wild for those of us used to the south," she said. Her voice was slow and soothing, and only one who knew her well would have recognised that her veneer of civility was not sincere. Mama was always in high spirits, and when she made such dull observations in a tone of voice reserved for prayer, it was always because she meant to stop an argument.

Her tone did not have its desired effect. Louisa-Margaretta said without a hint of a smile, "Yes, there are many walks that are solitary, and that is about all they have to recommend them."

"I am sure that you will have to find something else, because I shall insist that you accompany me the next time I am in the mood for some sort of exercise," said the Duke, who had not given them any reason to think he enjoyed either fresh air or exercise for the whole of his visit.

"As I said, sir, the walks are only pleasant if one is alone."

"I am sure you would not be so ungracious as to refuse me your company, Miss Haddington," he said. There was ever so slight an emphasis on the "Miss" in that sentence, and Louisa-Margaretta could not be sure whether the Duke was meaning to draw attention to her status as a spinster or simply to contrast his own titled person with Louisa-Margaretta's humbler station as a young lady who was merely rich.

"I am sure you would not be so ungracious as to insist on accompanying me," she said. "My first refusal is enough, surely."

Mr Galpin, who had been rather slumped in his own chair, straightened up to stare at Louisa-Margaretta. Gasps came from more than one quarter, and Louisa-Margaretta found that she had betrayed all of her earnest promises to the Countess, as well as more than one vow to herself. She had vowed that she would make her family proud and give nobody a reason to be ashamed of her conduct. Instead, she had offended their visitor, and the Duchess looked so pale as to be near swooning. Perhaps she had never heard a social inferior of her husband speak so boldly.

The Duke, for once, seemed to be without a response, so Louisa-Margaretta took the moment to excuse herself.

"I will return in one moment. I pray you would excuse me," she said, directing her words toward her mother. She did not need to ask the Duke to excuse her. But she saw how her mother had gone very still, and she knew that her parents would be angry.

She needed a moment to consider how she could win them back over. They had a right to be furious about many things she had done, but she knew in her heart the Duke deserved to hear a woman speak to him without the honeyed insincerity that he surely saw as his due.

25

———

By the time Louisa-Margaretta went down in the evening, she had thought of a plan of attack. She would have to use her words against the Duke more gently, with a cleverness that must be entirely disguised. If he had any sense that she was mocking him, he would make her pay for it. The man, while brutish, was not nearly as stupid as he usually appeared.

Her plan went wrong nearly from the start. Louisa-Margaretta was seated next to her father, which was not quite right in terms of the proper order of seating. They were supposed to be sitting in order of prominence, and Louisa-Margaretta was usually at the lowest end of the list. It suited her, because that was where Judith fell, so the two of them were able to speak freely. Of course, on that evening, it wouldn't have mattered, as Judith wasn't present, and she probably wouldn't have wished to speak to Louisa-Margaretta if she had been. But that day, Louisa-Margaretta was following just after her father, and as soon as he started in on her, she knew it must be one of Mama's schemes.

"Lou," he said in gentle tones. He was the only person

who ever used that name for her, as Mama always insisted on full names for the children. She had been the one to choose the names, after all, and she favored names that were elegant and difficult—Augustus, Sherborne, Percival, Loftus, and the most ornate name of all for her only daughter, Louisa-Margaretta. But Papa would rebel gently, when his wife was not near or when he'd had more than his usual measure of wine on a very special occasion. She was "Lou," and her brothers became either "Boy" or tender variations of their names—Perce, Sher, Loffie, Aug. "What's this I hear about you and our Miss St Clair?"

Louisa-Margaretta thought it was droll that her father referred to her friend that way. He greatly respected Judith, she knew, and had even gone so far as to defend her against some of Mama's accusations. But every time Judith was with them, Papa was even more silent than usual. He had never quite gotten used to making conversation with the rector or his daughter and seemed so intimidated by them that Louisa-Margaretta had to conclude he was even more God-fearing than his vocally religious wife.

"Nothing, Papa," she said. "I do not know why Mama did not think to invite her."

He had half a smile on his face, though it was strained. "Usually, you invite her, Lou. Your mother can't hope to stop you, even when it's not a good time to have her here."

For a moment, Louisa-Margaretta was warmed by the truth of that. At first, she and Judith had come together over their own objections. She'd thought Judith dull and priggish, and in her worst moments, she still did. Judith, who was an eternal diplomat around most of her father's parishioners, could not hide her opinion of Louisa-Margaretta. She thought her rich new neighbour spoiled, senseless, and hardly worth knowing. And Louisa-Margaretta knew that the question of riches still divided them. The only difference now was that Judith spoke her mind, and the two of them were mostly happy when they argued. Even when things were unsettled, they knew they were able to rely on each other.

Louisa-Margaretta pushed those thoughts aside. If she let Judith come closer to her, Judith might learn her secret. And though Judith had not approved of Mr Fortescue, she would be even more stern when it came to Mr Chandler. After all, he was married, and so Louisa-Margaretta was playing the role of a scarlet woman in drawing him away from the vows he had made before God and the church.

"She is occupied with her family," said Louisa-Margaretta. "And she hates our esteemed guests as much as I do."

The conversations around them were lively and loud, and Louisa-Margaretta had spoken quietly, but her father shook his head. "You ought never to say such things."

She glared at him. "Well, if I cannot say anything, I suppose I will not speak at all." And defiant, she took a most unladylike gulp of wine. She drank more wine than she ought through the rest of the meal, making desultory conversation with Mademoiselle Chatel about each dish and shocking her father into silence.

By the time the meal was over, Louisa-Margaretta had to make some effort to walk gracefully. But the wine had not improved her spirits. On the contrary, she felt very cross that the effect all the poets spoke of was not present at all. She felt no love, no great desire to sit and speak of the glories of nature, only a sour sensation in her gut and a hope that the quantity of wine she had taken would go undiscovered. After they finished eating, Cousin Morgan accosted her as the ladies and gentlemen were separating.

"What news do you have of Judith?" he asked.

"You ought not to call her that," said Louisa-Margaretta, enjoying the sensation of telling someone else what not to say. "It is... not proper."

She concentrated carefully to make sure that all of her words had their consonants and vowels in the proper places.

"Never mind that," he urged her. "Is she still cross with me? Why did she not come tonight?"

"All you men want to talk about is Miss St Clair," she said. "You have never even thought to ask me how I myself am faring, Cousin Morgan."

"I am sorry," he said without asking Louisa-Margaretta how she was. "But is Judith ill, or did she refuse to come tonight?"

"Why must you assume that I invited her?" asked Louisa-Margaretta, gazing in the direction that the ladies had gone. She did not long to join her mother, the Duchess, and the Chatel ladies. They would be a reminder of how much more interesting the evening might be were Judith there to join them.

"Please," he said. "I know I have offended her, going to the rectory as I did. But she has left me no choice. She has not given word to anyone in her family."

"You had every choice," snapped Louisa-Margaretta. "You could have let her tell them in her own time or let her change her mind and break off the engagement without causing a scandal. But instead, you trespass on our family's hospitality, abandon your studies, and try to force Judith's hand. Can you wonder that she is cross?"

The point was entirely lost on Cousin Morgan, and he trembled. Louisa-Margaretta felt unsteady that she had caused him such distress, but she did not take back her words.

"You think she means to break it off?" he asked.

Louisa-Margaretta sighed. Her head was hurting, and she could not tell whether it was from the wine or from her cousin's stupidity. "I thought you meant to break it off if she did not tell her family soon."

"What? Did she say that?"

"You must speak with her, not with me," said Louisa-Margaretta, and when he tried to insist, she shook her head. "No. It is for Judith to decide."

"I should have known you would not help me," he said, and she glared at him.

"No, I will not. Who are you that you should ask for my help? The fault is yours, and so must the remedy be."

"Cousin," he said, and she could tell that she had angered him, but she was thinking only of how she might walk away with a steady gait and a calm expression. If she was going to be sick, she needed to make her excuses to her mother as soon as she possibly could.

But Mama had other plans for her. As soon as she made her way into the little parlor where the ladies had gathered, Mama drew her near the fire and started murmuring.

"Louisa-Margaretta," she said, "I wish for all of our guests to feel welcome."

"I know," said Louisa-Margaretta, her resolve already abandoned. "You wish for me to apologize to the Duke. Have no fear. I shall be a simpering little simpleton around him in all future conversations."

"No," said her mother. "Of course, you ought to be kind to our guests, but it is Madame Chatel whose pardon you need to beg. You have been so rude to her that she now refuses to ask for your help, and when her own daughter is occupied, it is difficult for her to paint without anyone to assist."

"Did you not say she used to have no money? I am sure she will find some way to manage."

"Louisa-Margaretta," Mama said. "I am not making a request. I am giving you an order."

Louisa-Margaretta almost laughed. "Indeed, Mama? And shall I be whipped if I do not choose to follow it?"

Mama was not laughing. "We came here for you. And we gave Mr St Clair a living, and we stayed near Manchester for your father."

Louisa-Margaretta drew in a breath, clearheaded for the first time. The feeling that had come over her when she was with Cousin Morgan, that she might be sick at any moment, was gone. What her mother said to her was so shocking that she could not even consider her own reaction.

"Are you saying that you would take away Mr St Clair's living, Mama?" she said. "Send his family out in the cold, destroy Judith's marriage prospects, all because I will not flatter that interfering painter your friend invited to our home?"

"I am saying," said her mother, "that it is essential for you to remember your role in this family. Life is not simply a series of tedious obligations to be dodged at any cost and days in which we ought only to seek pleasure."

Louisa-Margaretta blinked. "Why would I make such a claim? I take no pleasure in anything now."

Mama, instead of her usual overflowing sympathy, showed only a stern expression to her daughter. "Then you ought to try meeting your obligations. Perhaps something more meaningful than pleasure will follow."

Louisa-Margaretta tried not to blush. Surely, Mama could know nothing of Mr Chandler, so she must be speaking of some other shortcoming. She looked at the other ladies, who were conversing, though the Duchess had an empty expression, and Mademoiselle Chatel spoke only every couple of minutes. Madame Chatel, resplendent in her usual white muslin, was speaking of the "old masters" of painting. Louisa-Margaretta felt a flash of real hatred for the woman. She made such a show of wearing only "simple" clothes, like her elegant muslin dresses, and of caring "not at all" for fine food or comfortable surroundings. And yet the way in which she spent her days, flattering royalty and painting them in the loveliest light possible, spoke of very different tastes.

"Yes," hissed Louisa-Margaretta. "I will go flatter our guests. I am sure they would enjoy nothing more than my contributions to this charming little conversation."

Mama, instead of responding to her daughter's tone, nodded solemnly. "You may find yourself surprised at the result."

26

Nothing about her conversations with the Chatels and the Duchess had been surprising to Louisa-Margaretta. Her humour had worsened during the course of the evening, but she felt she had put on a rather good show. She had managed it only because of the threat against Judith. She did not know if she would ever reconcile with Miss St Clair, but it would be mad for the poor rector to lose his living simply because Louisa-Margaretta would not bend to her mother's will.

For one moment, Louisa-Margaretta wondered what had come over Mama. She had always seemed to feel a certain affinity for the rector. True, his mild-mannered ways were very different from those of the iron-willed Mrs Haddington. Mama was born into an old, well-regarded family who had been "in need of funds" but never poor, and she had made a marriage that was exceptional both in terms of fortune and genuine affection, though Papa was not from the "right" sort of family. She had always been used to getting her way, never truly meeting her match until Louisa-Margaretta began to rebel against the circumstances of her own fortunate birth. Mama could be oblivious at times to the impact her actions had on other people's fortunes. For example, she might urge a farmer to give meat to a poor family, not thinking that the farmer himself had children to feed. But she had never yet threatened Louisa-Margaretta by implying that she might take away another family's income. Perhaps, at last, she had realised that no other threats would produce any effect. If only she had known how much Louisa-Margaretta desired her regard, and how much her dismissive comments to Madame Chatel had stung her daughter, she might have acted differently.

But Louisa-Margaretta was not about to tell her mother that.

She did not know how long she could play at behaving perfectly with their guests. After all, she had promised the Countess quite faithfully that she would flatter the Duke and Duchess and do nothing that would make the Countess or her husband ashamed of recommending Wycliff Castle, and she had not kept that promise for even a week. Now she was going to be expected to "assist" Madame Chatel as the woman painted portrait after insipid portrait.

Louisa-Margaretta decided not to admit that she envied the woman's skill. For if Madame Chatel had turned her hand to a different kind of painting, even something like Mr Chandler's more artistic landscapes, Louisa-Margaretta knew that the result would have been very impressive. Madame Chatel was more skilled than anyone Louisa-Margaretta had ever seen. And for all her pleas for assistance with the more tedious parts of her work, the Frenchwoman was extremely industrious.

Mr Chandler was never far from Louisa-Margaretta's thoughts. She remembered him in the morning as soon as she awoke, her mouth dry and her head crawling with pain.

Eating would be impossible, yet some part of her was hungry. She was also transported by thoughts of Mr Chandler. Though it was unspeakable, and she could not even admit her desires to herself, she was still drawn to him. Perhaps, in comparison to the way she had once felt about Isaac, Mr Chandler was a troubling and pitiful substitute. But if she was never to have any luck in love, and she had to spend all of her time pretending to be a gracious little lady, she must have something of her own in life. Back in Essex, that had taken the form of work, but now she was not to be allowed even that measure of dignity.

Louisa-Margaretta found herself dressing, leaving the house, and getting a horse from the stables. Let them think she had gone for a ride. She need not have any pretenses about sketching any longer. Since wine did not give her any oblivion and made it even harder to endure the visitors, she must have something to take the sharpness out of the many ways in which her life had disappointed her.

Before she knew it, she was at the beautiful spot over-looking the lake. Their stable master, perhaps sensing Louisa-Margaretta's mood, had given her the ill-tempered mare named Godiva, and Louisa-Margaretta took advantage of all the horse's speed. Godiva was difficult to handle but, once urged into a pace she liked, became a rather impressive horse.

Louisa-Margaretta was reminded of the times she had ridden Godiva, and other horses, with more of a purpose. She and Judith had once found ways of making their minds useful, and while she did not wish any more scandal on her family, she could not help noticing that she and her friend created trouble when none came to them. Well, Judith did not, though Louisa-Margaretta knew that even a clergyman's daughter might tend to grow tired of constantly abiding by others' rules, both religious and societal. But Louisa-Margaretta could not abide boredom. When there were others worse off than her, as there had been during her brief time outside London the year before, she was able to forget her troubles for a time. Indeed, Judith had also thrived when given such responsibilities. But in the empty passages of Wycliff Castle, with duties that did not go beyond making amends for the offense she had caused the Duke? Louisa-Margaretta was like Godiva herself, who kicked and bit all the more when she was confined and forced into idleness.

For Mr Chandler was trouble. She could not pretend otherwise. Louisa-Margaretta knew from personal experience that those who were indiscreet were always discovered. She was fortunate that the only tidings to have reached her family's ears concerning Mr Fortescue were rumours, and Louisa-Margaretta had confirmed that he was interested but strenuously denied that she had ever been alone with him, much less that she had gone alone to his London house. They did not know that he still had a hold over her.

She made Godiva run still faster. Mr Fortescue's threats were always with her, never quite extinguished by Judith's reassurances. Louisa-Margaretta did feel a bit of relief when she was far from London, as she knew Mr Fortescue hated both travel and the countryside. Also, he would not want to give her parents any cause to intervene. His aim had always been to convince her to marry him then present it all to the elder Haddingtons as a *fait accompli*. Demure Mr Haddington would not like it, but his hands would be tied if the banns had been read. After all, Louisa-Margaretta was of age, and by law, she could marry where she chose. That had been true for some years. At twenty-seven, she ought to have reached some pinnacle of freedom, but she could not feel it.

After all, freedom in marriage was of little use, since she could not marry Isaac. At least Mr Chandler, she thought, would make no such demands.

As Godiva came near the top of the rise, Louisa-Margaretta anticipated their meeting. She would never be a true prisoner as long as she had someone like Mr Chandler to amuse her, to remind her that at least part of her soul was still living. Perhaps nobody in her home understood her, and neither did he, but the more earthly delights formed some sort of shared understanding.

She got down from Godiva quickly, all at once ready to find Mr Chandler and begin, without pretense, to make her wishes known, when an unfamiliar voice stopped her.

"Oh, I would not," said the voice, cheerful in its warning. "It would be most unwise."

27

Judith went to help her father, who wished to rearrange some things in the pews in anticipation of their esteemed visitors. Though none of them had shown any intention of coming to church so far, especially not the papist Madame Chatel, Judith thought she might be able to convince the Duchess to come. It would mean trying to go to Wycliff Castle without seeing Louisa-Margaretta, which would be a challenge, but perhaps she might slip in and out while her friend was riding. For she had no doubt that Louisa-Margaretta would be cantering over the hills by then, likely on some horrid horse like that spiteful Godiva. And she would be wishing for a shooting party, though with only her father and the Duke on hand, it would be a sad little company. Judith knew that Morgan did not like to shoot.

Thinking of Morgan, she shivered. The gall! He would come all the way to Derbyshire then not bother to come see her, even after intruding on her family. One of the things Judith had always loved about him was that he understood her. Unlike Louisa-Margaretta, he never demanded that she explain her disposition or her place in the world. But the engagement had ruined things. For then, they were always talking at cross purposes, whether in letters or in person, and she wondered with a heavy heart whether it portended ill if they could somehow still marry.

"Papa," she said, so softly that she hoped her father would not hear. He had been walking between the pews toward the vestry, but he hesitated when she spoke.

"Yes, Judith?"

He walked over to her, and all at once, she nearly lost her nerve. His gaze was so open, so sincere! *What will he think when he finds that I have betrayed him with a secret engagement?*

"I must..." she said then only blinked at her father. "Papa."

"Judith." He had the good grace not to be too amused but simply stood still and waited for her. Another person would have turned the conversation or demanded to know what she was thinking or gone off to find some other occupation. But Judith's father had been a clergyman long enough that he knew when someone had an important message to deliver. He would give Judith time to speak, and she found it galling, for she hated breaking his trust.

They were interrupted by the sound of little footsteps.

"Judith, Moses and Aaron will not let me play soldiers with them!" cried little Joseph, grabbing Judith's hand.

Papa gave a very slight smile. His children were not permitted to play soldiers at all, and if Joseph were not such an uncommonly guileless child, he would have thought to omit the nature of their game from his complaint.

"What does Miriam say?" asked Judith.

Joseph knew that he was not to fling things about in a sacred space, but he stamped hard on the floor a few times.

"Nothing. She is with the Chandlers again. They were supposed to all go sketching together, so she told me not to bother you or Papa, and she took her sketching things with her."

Judith could not then hide her smile, though she could not tell whether she was truly amused or only relieved. "Perhaps we should go out as well. Would you like to visit the Fletchers? I will walk there with you."

Joseph ran about the village constantly, but recently, the distance between him and Moses and Aaron had widened so much that he had started to cling to his father and sisters. His brothers, at nine and ten, had little patience for a boy who worshipped them, and Judith hoped that the attention of his friends in the village would be enough to soothe Joseph's temper. Of late, he had been frustrated with his brothers for what seemed like every minute of every day, and it had begun to wear on the whole family.

"I can walk with Joseph," said Papa. "Judith, you have a visitor."

The door to the church, which was often kept unlocked, opened. The cold air blew in with Louisa-Margaretta, who looked pink from the cold and uncommonly tired.

"Mr St Clair!" she said. "Ju— Miss St Clair. I am sorry. I did not expect to find anyone here."

"We are often working in here during the day," said Judith, straightening her stance. "But we can leave, if you wish."

Louisa-Margaretta looked confused, and Papa patted Judith's arm. "Not to worry, my dear. I will walk Joseph over to the Fletchers. You may stay with your friend."

As they made their way to the door, Judith heard Joseph saying, "I can go, Papa! You are so slow," and taking off at a run. The rector followed his son out and closed the door delicately, leaving only Judith and Louisa-Margaretta.

They were silent for a moment, then Judith asked Louisa-Margaretta about the guests. "Could you invite Mademoiselle Chatel and the Duchess to come here? It would be terribly rude if nobody at all came to church, even if Madame Chatel is a Catholic."

Louisa-Margaretta nodded. "Yes. I think the Duchess will probably come. Mama could convince anyone."

They were silent again, then Judith nodded. "Well, then. I must go speak to my brothers. Unless you needed something?"

She had asked only for the sake of politeness, but Louisa-Margaretta swallowed. "There is some kind of saint, is there not? A patron saint of lost causes? Would that be Saint Augustine?"

Judith frowned. She had never known her friend to display any interest in religion. In fact, Louisa-Margaretta cared so little about the church that she was constantly scolding Judith for not becoming a Quaker so that she might easily marry Morgan.

"It is Saint Jude," she said cautiously. "Thaddeus, not Iscariot. But I am sure you know we do not pray to saints."

"Yes," said Louisa-Margaretta absently, her eyes wandering over to the windows. "Praying to saints. Pardon?"

Judith did not know what to make of her friend's confusion, much less of her desire to pray in a church. Though the chapel at Wycliff Castle was little used, as Mrs Haddington preferred to come to the church or pray in whichever room happened to please her, Judith knew that the room was well stocked with candles and very clean. Louisa-Margaretta had no need at all to leave her home, and Judith was surprised to see her so distraught.

However, she was certainly able to enlighten her friend on the point of praying to Saint Jude. "Invocation of saints is a fond thing, vainly invented and grounded upon no warranty of Scripture but rather repugnant to the Word of God," said Judith.

"What?" Louisa-Margaretta looked briefly at Judith before turning her head again.

"This is one of the Thirty-Nine Articles," said Judith. "One of the basic tenets of our faith, as it were."

"But do you believe it? Never mind," said Louisa-Margaretta hastily. "It should follow that I am not allowed to pray to such a saint. I am not sure even Saint Jude would wish to contend with my troubles."

And she rushed outside again, leaving the door half open.

Judith sighed as she took hold of the door to close it, watching her friend yank Godiva's bridle from the branch where she had tied it tight. Louisa-Margaretta, tired of entertaining trying guests, had apparently found that even spiritual pursuits were less tedious than what propriety demanded. That reminded Judith why she could not stand to be around her friend at times. Judith, bereft of her mother and tasked with caring for her entire family, felt that she had genuine troubles. Louisa-Margaretta, were she half as spoiled, would have no troubles at all.

Judith had no sooner closed the door than it was opened again, that time by her father.

"I saw Miss Haddington leaving," he said. "I wish I could have spoken to her. Has there been some sort of difficulty at Wycliff Castle?"

"No," said Judith.

"You are sure, dear?"

Judith moved away from the doorway. "She came

because she wanted to pray to St Jude. Imagine, with all of her mother's religious instruction, she did not know that we never pray to saints!"

Her father gave a sad smile, gesturing toward one of the older pews. Judith went in, and he sat with her.

"*We* do not pray to saints, my dear," he said. "But you must have noticed that many of my parishioners do. Indeed, it has always been so."

"But you correct them," Judith insisted. "If one of them says that they are going to pray to Saint Francis, you say that we will offer up a prayer to God, thinking of Saint Francis, who is in heaven."

"My dear," said Papa, "of course I do. But surely you can see that this is a change in the words only. I am quite sure that most people who hear my prayers address their own directly to Saint Francis, not to God."

"But that is heresy!"

Papa nodded. "Perhaps. But much of what we do may be heresy, my dear. God does not ask us to go beyond our own understanding. We try to understand what He wishes and to follow what we understand him to have set out for us, but we are bound to err."

"So we may as well be Papists ourselves, then?"

"No, Judith. But I do not doubt the sincerity of their faith, nor do I doubt your friend's intentions. You were sure that she was well? Nothing has happened to her since the visitors came?"

Judith stared at her father, who was sitting in the pew and asking for details of a private conversation just like any of his gossiping parishioners. Something in his tone told her he did not ask for his own gratification. Her father was strongly opposed to gossip, always counseling that they were permitted to seek such information only as would enable them to do good.

And in fact, something about Louisa-Margaretta had given Judith pause. Even though Louisa-Margaretta was often dull or out of spirits when forced to do things she did not like, some part of her spirit had seemed to be entirely missing. And Judith's father was asking whether something had happened at Wycliff Castle as if he expected a misfortune to befall them. Papa, though absent-minded enough, was a very keen judge of character, and it appeared he had seen more in Louisa-Margaretta's distracted air than Judith had been able to find.

"Papa," she said, her voice full of caution. "You speak as if you expected some sad news from Wycliff Castle."

Her father stood and went out of the pew. He walked so quickly about the church that Judith almost thought she had offended him. After he had opened the doors to both the outside and vestry then closed them again, he came back to the pew.

"You are old enough to hear my thoughts on this matter, Judith," he said. "You have been of age for some time, I suppose. But your mother always thought it better that I not share them. This was for your sake, you understand."

Judith, remembering her mother, felt both grief and elation. For it was only Papa and Miriam who shared her memories to such an extent that they could speak in such a way. Moses and Aaron had known their mother in the way that small children could, and Joseph had fewer memories still. But Judith, Miriam, and Papa had all known the wise, clever woman who waited for them all in heaven. Most of the stories they shared were full of tenderness and humour, but Judith knew at once that the one she was about to hear would be different.

"If Mama thought you should not tell me," said Judith with some force of will, "then perhaps it is right that you stay silent. I will not press you."

She would, though. Once her father had revealed the idea of a secret, she wished to know, especially since it might concern the Haddingtons.

He sighed. "There are many points on which we did not agree... That is, in terms of what we shared with you. I have always been inclined to go along with your mother's wishes, my dear, but on this, I believe I cannot stay silent. If she knew that Louisa-Margaretta was threatened by her ignorance, I am sure she would agree with me."

"Threatened?" said Judith.

"Perhaps that is not the right word," said Papa, responding to the fear in Judith's features. "But my dear, I was not sure how much to say before. There are many reasons that I have requested that neither you nor Miriam visit Wycliff Castle during this time. Perhaps it was too much to expect that you would respect this wish without understanding any of the concerns behind it."

Judith felt a rush of shame. Not only had she gone against her father's wishes in forming a secret engagement, which she had still not managed to reveal to him, but she had disobeyed him and gone over to the Haddingtons whenever she could manage it. Judith had behaved as if she were still permitted to go to the grand home whenever she pleased, acting with all of the presumptuousness and greed of a poor relation. She knew that her papa never forbade her from doing anything and had not only taken her on visits to unseemly places such as poorhouses and prisons but had actively encouraged her to take up work in Essex that any other clergyman might have found unsuitable for his daughter. And yet when he warned her against going to visit Louisa-Margaretta, she had not given his words any thought. Perhaps she was still ignorant of the dangers, but it might be too late for her friend.

"Is it something about Madame Chatel?" she asked. "Do you suspect her of stealing the paintings, that she might profit off doing the Duke's portrait herself?"

"Judith," said her father, "of course not! I would never make such a fuss over something so small as the theft of a portrait."

"Small," breathed Judith. She had not been in London during the thefts, of course, but she had some sense of the very great scandal they had caused. "Such a thing is certainly not small!"

"An offense against property, Judith. It is still a sin, but in our society, theft has been elevated to a position it does not deserve. It is far graver moral danger that I see here."

Judith began to speak, but her father held up a hand.

"No, let me speak, my dear. You ought to hear my views on the monarchy but only if you are prepared never to repeat them. Not to your most intimate friends, your husband, even your sister."

"H-Husband?" stammered Judith.

"Yes, when you marry," said Papa, oblivious to her unease. "There were no secrets between your mother and me, and that is allowable. But when you do marry, I should not wish for you to put the fellow in a difficult position, which you would do if you expressed my sentiments faithfully."

Judith breathed again. He had not been speaking of Morgan specifically, only he assumed that she would marry. It was rather a touching certainty, as Judith knew she was of an age and fortune that meant spinsterhood was a rather wiser supposition.

"Yes," she said. "I will share nothing, Papa. If Louisa-Margaretta must be warned, let me find a way to do it without alarming her."

"Very well," he said. "I must begin with a story."

And Judith listened. It was the other half of a story that she remembered from her Mama. There was Awellah, the young girl who was large with child when the banns were read. Even then, Judith had known that the young man in the village who married Awellah was not the child's natural father. But because Judith's parents had helped Awellah marry quickly, the little girl was spared the shame of illegitimacy. The man who raised her was her legal father.

But what Judith had never known was that Awellah had been violated. When she was working as a servant in a very rich household, one of the young men had a reputation. He was not only debauched but also violent. And when Awellah spoke of the young man's crime to her employers, she was dismissed without a reference.

"And the person who did it?" asked Judith, breathless. "Was it the Duke, do you think?"

"No, my dear," her father said gently. "This was many years ago, when the Duke was not yet born."

Judith frowned. "Then why tell me this story?"

"Because the Duke has come from the same people, the same upbringing. He was surely taught that he deserved respect but that he had no obligation to show respect to people who are not of noble birth. I cannot say whether any of the rumours about his conduct are true, but even if they are not, his lack of kindness to his hosts sets a very poor example."

"The rumours?"

Judith should have known before asking that her father was not going to tell her. He only shook his head.

"They are unproven, and I will not slander him," he said. "But to me, it seemed wise to warn you and Miriam away from that place. I warned the Haddingtons, too, but they did not believe me."

"Whyever not?" asked Judith, incredulous. "Louisa-Margaretta is their princess. Surely, they wished only to protect her."

Her father gave a sad smile. "I believe they thought that this visit would protect her reputation. And Mrs Haddington got a recommendation from an intimate friend of hers, Countess Koltsova. She was not inclined to distrust it."

Judith wondered about her friend's strange behavior. "Can we trust anything that others tell us, Papa?"

"Trust in God, my dear," he said, as she knew that he would. As they prayed together, Judith's mind wandered back to Wycliff Castle. She felt that she could not be easy until the Duke, and all who had accompanied him, left Derbyshire for good. But she did not know how to force them out, especially when neither Louisa-Margaretta nor Mrs Haddington would look kindly on her interference.

28

Louisa-Margaretta felt weary when she arrived at Wycliff Castle. As soon as she passed through its large doors, she wondered whether she might manage to get to her room while avoiding both her mother's relentless energy and the scrutiny of their guests.

As usual, she was unable to sneak off. Mama was upon her without warning, steering her toward the Cabinet Library and a man with cold eyes.

"My dear," she said, "Mr Fletcher wishes to speak with all of us. Thank you for coming home as soon as our terrible news reached you."

Louisa-Margaretta was not going to correct her mother. "Yes, Mama," she said while trying to place the man. For she must have been introduced to Mr Fletcher at some point, though she could not think when. She remembered hearing that he was a man of frugal habits and rather extensive property, though nothing compared to what the Haddingtons could command.

Judith had visited the family more often and spoken of the strange pattern that they followed. "Sour, sweet, sour, sweet" was a little phrase that had gone about the village in order to make gossiping about the sons easier. And certainly, it did fit them rather perfectly. Mrs Fletcher's eldest son, a product of her first marriage, was profligate and ill-tempered. He was succeeded by a brother who was quiet and intelligent. After those young men were born, Mrs Fletcher had been widowed, and so over a decade followed before she married again. She promptly had two more sons. The first son she had with Mr Fletcher was a wild boy, the second a sweet little cherub. Though Louisa-Margaretta seldom took an interest in children, even she had been amazed by the contrast between the two little boys. Though she was rather different from her brothers, still they were all full of opinions and life. There was not the same extreme division that she saw in each set of Fletcher boys.

Behind those contrasts, Mr Fletcher himself was hardly a remarkable presence. Louisa-Margaretta had been vaguely aware that he was magistrate. When Mama had gone on about how she tried diligently to ensure that local lads were not punished unfairly for minor offenses, Louisa-Margaretta never listened at all. It went sorely against the grain that her mother would not approve a marriage that, while unconventional, would certainly be respectable, yet she believed so strongly that local lads ought to be able to steal pheasants. Mama fired every gamekeeper her husband had ever engaged, so adamantly did she believe in letting those little thefts go unpunished.

"Well, then," said Mr Fletcher. He left a very long pause. He did not beg Louisa-Margaretta's pardon or clear his throat or avert his eyes. He certainly did not invite her to be seated, which would have been the polite thing, so they stood staring at each other like actors on a stage. Even in the very first part of their conversation, Louisa-Margaretta sensed that he would not be the easiest mark.

Still, she hoped that respect for her family's position would win over whatever petty concern had brought him to their home. "It is wonderful to see you, Mr Fletcher. I pray you would excuse me. It has been a rather tiring day."

"Oh?" he said. "May I ask why, Miss Haddington? Where have you spent the day?"

Louisa-Margaretta could only look to her mother, but the rudeness of the inquiry had not registered with Mama.

"Indeed, my dear," Mrs Haddington said. "I know that you told me of your plans, but I confess that the events of the day have made my memory rather shaky."

Louisa-Margaretta began to laugh then suppressed it as soon as she saw her mother's face. Indeed, Mama's memory never erred in the slightest. She was unfailingly precise in her recollections, though perhaps she did not wish Mr Fletcher to know that Louisa-Margaretta had gone off alone without so much as consulting either of her parents.

"I went out sketching," she said. "That is, I meant to sketch."

She had realised that she had not brought a satchel with her, though she might have given it to a servant.

Mr Fletcher nodded politely, refusing to look away, and she cleared her throat.

"By the time, erm, I found that I had nothing with me," she said, "well, I decided to go to the church to pray."

"Why?"

His questions were getting even more impertinent. She straightened.

"My friend Miss St Clair has influenced me in this practise," she said. "Miss St Clair is a very, erm, quite a good influence. Spiritually, indeed."

Mama joined her. "Oh yes. Miss St Clair is very pious, and she has brought the rest of us into a proper frame of mind."

Louisa-Margaretta could not keep her lips from twitching. All that from Mama, who had spent months trying to wrest her away from Judith's friendship! For Mama to be coming out with such wild untruths, the situation must be serious indeed.

"Thank you, dear," said Mama when Mr Fletcher made no reply. "I'm sure you can go and prepare now. We must have something to eat for the guests, even if nobody is thinking of it."

"One more minute, Miss Haddington, if you would be so kind," said Mr Fletcher. His words, once again, were at odds with his appearance. He plainly meant to keep Louisa-Margaretta, even if she was not feeling kindly disposed toward him.

"Mr Fletcher," she said. "I beg your pardon, but my mother is perfectly correct. Our hospitality and duty to our guests must come first, much as I would like to stay and chat."

For the first time, the man looked angry, though he then composed his features back into their mask of cold formality.

"I would agree with that, Miss Haddington," he said. "But one cannot think too much about hospitality when one of those very guests has been murdered."

Judith heard the news from her brothers. They spent so much time with servants that they were the surest source of village gossip. Her father also tended to hear things quickly, but unlike his sons, he was seldom willing to share other families' news without a specific purpose.

Aaron had no such discretion. "Another murder at Wycliff Castle! It must be full of ghosts!"

"Aaron," said Miriam. "Nobody believes in ghosts."

"I believe in ghosts," said Moses, looking worried, but after a glance from his older brother, he quickly changed his opinion. "And I'm not scared! It's the Haddingtons who should be afraid. The spirits will all haunt them."

Joseph's lip trembled.

"Moses," Judith said gently. Usually, he was responsive to the note of warning in her voice, but he ignored it that time.

"And they will rise from their graves," said Aaron.

"Aaron," said Judith, more snappish. "I shall have to tell Papa."

"No," said Moses, drawing the word out. "You won't, because you don't like to trouble him."

Judith frowned. "That is true, but he would not like such talk. For he knows these spirits do not exist, and it is cruel to pretend such a thing."

"I'm not pretending," said Aaron, clearly offended by the accusation.

"You have an excellent imagination," said Judith firmly, looking to Miriam for help, but her sister only laughed.

"I never did!" said Aaron, indignant.

"Nor I!" insisted Moses.

"That is completely untrue," said Judith, nearly in tears. That her brothers should wish to be dullards, bound only by fact and not by any sort of creativity, seemed somehow even more tragic than the idea of them discussing such a sordid topic as murder. Joseph, who had been troubled by the talk of violence, frowned as he saw the argument escalating.

"It is not," insisted Aaron, and Miriam shook her head.

"Boys!" she said. "At attention!"

Aaron, Moses, and Joseph were silent. They stood in a line.

"Salute to the king," said Miriam, her clear voice perfectly audible above the noise of the fire.

All three saluted, and she nodded solemnly. "Now, outside and march."

Moses began to say something, but she said, "Silence, soldier! Not until you finish your maneuvers."

Judith watched in astonishment as all three of her brothers marched out of the room.

"They will be no trouble now, so long as they don't all collapse into anarchy while getting their coats," said

Miriam, lolling about on the sofa. "Ah, how lovely it is to have this room to ourselves again!"

"Why did they listen to you?" asked Judith.

"It is only a little game we all have. 'Army' is what we call it."

"But Papa will be furious! He hates when war is made into a game."

"Then he is welcome to shepherd our brothers about," said Miriam. "Honestly, Judith, he never notices a thing. And neither do you. We have been playing this game for a year, since you were gone and after you came back, and this is the first time you have remarked on it."

Judith frowned. "But why have them play when Papa hates it so?"

"They love it! Besides, it is the only way to get them to listen. They will not listen to their sister else."

"They listen to me."

Miriam laughed. "Never! Just now, were they listening?"

Judith, rather than admitting the truth, pressed the point. "So they will listen to their colonel, then?"

Miriam scoffed. "Absolutely not. I am the general."

"The general!"

"Yes. I have promised Aaron or Moses that they might be promoted to colonel if I am impressed, but they keep failing in their duties to Lieutenant Joseph. I have had to punish them by keeping them in their current ranks."

Judith sighed. "I suppose it kept them from talking of the murder," she said rather grudgingly. "So, thank you."

"Yes." Miriam smiled. "And now they have gone, we can stop setting such a holy example and speak of it ourselves."

"You know of it?" asked Judith, despairing. It was all over the village. If the Haddingtons had ever had any hope of keeping it secret, that hope was lost.

"Oh, Judith," said Miriam. "I have hardly been cloistered myself! I was at the Chandlers', and we were hours waiting for Mr Chandler to come in. I have probably heard more than you have."

"We shouldn't speak of it," said Judith, but her voice was weak.

Miriam shrugged. "You will be worried about your friend. What is she going to do? With a scandal like this, the Haddingtons will have to leave Wycliff Castle."

"Surely not," said Judith, drawing in her breath. Not only would that be unfortunate for Louisa-Margaretta, who needed her hunting and long rides in the steep hills every bit as much as a country gentleman, but it would hurt her family even more.

Miriam sensed that answer. "Don't trouble yourself." She shook her head. "I'm sure the Haddingtons will find some way to provide for Papa."

Judith frowned. "I'm sure they do not care a great deal, Miriam. The parish needed a rector, and Mrs Haddington chose Papa for the position, which has turned out very well for her. If we are to have new patrons, they may wish to bestow the living on someone else. At the very least, they may feel that Papa's compensation is far too generous."

"It is not!" said Miriam. "Mr Barnwell had to come on as a curate because Papa nearly died fulfilling his duties!"

"Of course," said Judith patiently, "but another rich family might not feel the same way. They might not think Papa deserves a curate, for example."

Miriam bit her lip. "What I am telling you," she said, "is that the Haddingtons are not going to abandon Papa or our family."

"Mrs Haddington hates me," said Judith tonelessly. She had tried for months to pretend to her family that all was well, but the disturbing news from Wycliff Castle had flattened her. Her thoughts swirled into darkness, and she felt both uneasy and poor.

Miriam tossed her head. "She doesn't hate you, you sapscull. She is only cross because Louisa-Margaretta causes her so much heartache."

"It is not Louisa-Margaretta's fault," said Judith, trying to defend her friend without giving any specifics.

"That is what everyone says when a young lady is rich and beautiful," said Miriam with a bitterness Judith had seldom heard. "But Judith, what if someday, Louisa-Margaretta is forced to face the consequences of her recklessness? What then?"

30

———

ousin Morgan cornered her in the chapel. It was a strangely appropriate place for him to find her, as neither one of them liked to use that room. Louisa-Margaretta, without thinking of it, had repeated her steps from earlier in the day. But that time, instead of going to the modest church meant for all, she had made her way to Wycliff Castle's ornate chapel. It was not often used, as Mama liked to pray in all sorts of rooms and took considerable delight in overseeing many improvements at the church. Louisa-Margaretta often joked that a poor man in the village would sit in a better pew than a rich Londoner, though Judith did not find any of that particularly humorous. "And why should they not?" she would say. "For surely the poor deserve comfort when they worship."

Louisa-Margaretta thought the poor ought to be given the comfort of missing church entirely, but Judith had never shared that opinion.

When Louisa-Margaretta entered the chapel, the scent of cedar did something to calm her. Sitting before the altar, she did not achieve a state of divine contemplation, but her breathing slowed. She knew from her own experience that murder was alarming, but it did not always signify a greater danger. And, she thought, it was no wonder that somebody had killed the Duke. He seemed to go about making enemies, and surely some subversive from London might have followed him.

"Do you think I have a chance?" asked Cousin Morgan, sitting down beside her. "My dear cousin, I have offended Miss St Clair."

"So have I," said Louisa-Margaretta without thinking. "But I will need her help now. That is, if she will speak to either of us now that our house is beset by scandal."

"But of course she will!" said Cousin Morgan, his voice rising. "That is the thing about our dear Ju—about Miss St Clair. She is never offended by scandal and in fact very little interested in it."

Louisa-Margaretta gave a hollow laugh. "I suppose that is true. If she were truly afraid of such things, she would have ceased any friendship with me long ago."

She wondered if she ought to say so much. After all, Cousin Morgan was presumably still ignorant of everything that had passed between Louisa-Margaretta and Mr Chandler. If she had any hope of keeping it secret, she needed to ensure that she told nobody. Not her cousin, not her friend, not the most discreet soul on earth. In fact, she had to forget it herself, though the unease she felt meant she was hardly likely to forget it soon.

"Judith may have an idea," she added. "She always has a special sense when it comes to murder."

"What a horrid thing to say!"

"Cousin," snapped Louisa-Margaretta. "We have all had the unhappy experience of being rather close to more than one murder, though I am sure we might wish to forget. I am better at understanding the passions a murderer might feel —the hatred, the jealousy. But surely you remember that Judith is much better at discovering the material facts and sorting through them. If we are going to discover who killed the Duke, we will need her help."

Cousin Morgan turned white. "But should we go looking for that answer, Cousin Louisa-Margaretta? Perhaps it is best to mourn him quietly."

"Mr Fletcher will go looking for that answer," she snapped. "And he will keep asking me about my every thought and deed until he finds the person who is responsible."

Cousin Morgan gently put a hand on her arm. "Never mind that. But do you think Miss St Clair will speak to me? I am afraid I have offended her gravely, first by coming here then by visiting her home without her invitation. I had only hoped to make it easier for her to speak, but now I see I have done the opposite."

Louisa-Margaretta looked up at the detailed paintings on the ceiling of the chapel, concentrating on one particu-larly silly-looking cherub. Only a man in love would think that the outcome of his behavior to his fiancée must be more important than murder.

"You ought to go and ask her," she said, drawing her arm away. "What have I to do with it?"

"I cannot go now," he said. "If she is angry with me, I cannot force her to converse again. It was unkind to do so the first time. I see that now."

Louisa-Margaretta sighed. "So you wish me to represent your cause?"

"Yes," said her cousin. "No. But ask whether I will be welcome."

Louisa-Margaretta shook her head, smiling for the first

time that day. "Cousin Morgan, permit me to speak plainly. The two of you had much better marry and be done with it."

"Dost thou think she would marry me?" he asked, slipping into the plain speech favored by the Quakers.

At that, Louisa-Margaretta smiled wider. "I cannot make any promises. But I will speak with her. Heaven knows, if this event does not cause her to turn away from our family entirely, I cannot see a little theological disagreement making any difference."

She wondered if she had spoken too hastily, as Cousin Morgan looked rather too radiant for such a quiet, awkward man. But her heart was so heavy that she could not bear to undo his joy.

31

Louisa-Margaretta did not wait to be announced, sweeping into the room where Judith sat with her sister Miriam.

"Good morning," she said just as she would on an ordinary morning. "I hope I haven't disturbed you by calling."

"No indeed," said Miriam, her tones clipped. "I was just about to go see my friends the Chandlers. Louisa-Margaretta, I understand from them that you have taken up painting."

Louisa-Margaretta could not know how much Miriam knew, but instead of answering carefully, she said without thinking, "I did try, but I found it rather dull."

Miriam smiled, but Louisa-Margaretta did not detect anything mocking in the expression.

"Miss Chandler said she was surprised to see you at one of their favourite haunts."

Louisa-Margaretta nodded as firmly as she could manage. "They are welcome to that spot. I shan't be going there again. I find the whole business of sketching in autumn rather horrid. It's so cold and frosty that I may come away without one of my fingers if I attempt it again."

Judith looked from one to the other with a puzzled expression. Miriam did not look as if she perfectly understood Louisa-Margaretta, but she had continued to smile.

"Well, then," she said. "Enjoy your visit here. I am sure it will not end in any lost fingers."

After Miriam left the room, Judith turned toward Louisa-Margaretta.

"Please listen," she said. "I am sorry for what I said, but I cannot visit Wycliff Castle any longer."

"What?" said Louisa-Margaretta. "Of course you must."

"No," Judith said, her voice quieter. "I'm not going to give a reason, but I cannot. I am very sorry for what has happened to your family."

"Are you indeed?" asked Louisa-Margaretta, her temper rising. "We are once again suspected of murder, only this time, the magistrate is looking rather too closely at me. But I suppose you would just let me swing."

"That is not fair," said Judith, and something in her glare cowed Louisa-Margaretta. Judith could credibly claim that she would never let an innocent person be hanged. Louisa-Margaretta could not claim to be a defender of justice, not in the same way that Judith was. But she would be damned if she would allow the noose to tighten around her.

"Well, then," Louisa-Margaretta said. "If you will not come for war, come for love. My cousin would speak with you."

That had the intended effect. Judith stared at her friend then down at her hands. She went over to the pianoforte and began to play Bach but without the usual sureness of meter that defined her playing.

"You shan't escape me," said Louisa-Margaretta, easier

then. She stood next to the piano. "I have known men who are selfish, arrogant, anything but honorable," she said, growing cross with Judith. "And my cousin, though he seems like a dullard at times, is not any of those things. You may as well give him an audience."

"It's not a question of that," murmured Judith, continuing to play.

Louisa-Margaretta put her hands over her friend's. Judith stared at her in surprise.

"Cousin Morgan wishes to marry you," she said. "Say yes or no, but why should it trouble you to this degree?"

"Because I wanted nothing more than to marry him, until he came here," cried Judith. She snatched her hands away and put them over her face. "I cannot say now. If we cannot settle this simple matter of speaking to my family, how are we ever to manage many decades of marriage?"

Louisa-Margaretta felt ill. She did not think of marriage that way at all. Indeed, with Mr Fortescue, marriage would have been a punishment. With Isaac, it would have been heaven itself. Louisa-Margaretta could not conceive of Judith's hesitation in telling her family about the engagement. If Louisa-Margaretta herself were in Morgan's position, she would never accept such hesitation from a future spouse.

"You do not need to marry," she said swiftly. "Only speak with my poor cousin. He is quite losing his head."

Judith's voice trembled when she answered. "But how will I speak with him? I have no idea of what I should say."

Louisa-Margaretta waved her hand, batting away Judith's objections as if they were floating in the air. "Fine, then. You may have all day to think on it! But I do not have such leisure, so you must listen to me talk about this murderer."

She had tried to make her voice rich with bravery, yet

she was still scared. She and Judith, having encountered people desperate enough to murder before, knew just how much danger and fear one person could cause. Louisa-Margaretta did not know what it would take to keep her family safe, and Wycliff Castle had begun to feel oppressive again. It was so large, so full of places where a person or a painting might be hidden.

Judith stood, stepping away from the piano. "Let us go out. We would do better to walk."

32

───────

As soon as Judith and Louisa-Margaretta began their walk, Judith had cause to regret her decision. The wind had turned bitter, and Louisa-Margaretta's comment about losing a finger to the frost proved apt. The autumn in Derbyshire was supposed to be beautiful, but Judith had already found the weather far too cold. She always had trouble eating enough to have a strong, pleasing figure like her friend's and feared she was looking gaunt again. All of the sleep she had lost over her secret engagement was turning her into an old woman.

"I must improve on this cloak," Judith said as she tripped down the lane, struggling to keep pace with Louisa-Margaretta. "It is not nearly warm enough for autumn."

Her friend snorted. "Autumn in Derbyshire lasts all of two days," she noted. "It is always as hot as the devil here or so cold we shall all die of the chill."

"Much like your own temper," said Judith without thinking. She was surprised to find that she had still not quite forgiven Louisa-Margaretta's outburst of the other day.

But her friend only laughed. "Yes, much like my temper, may God help me! Listen to you, Judith. You have become quite a wit."

"I assure you I have not," said Judith, but she was clearly pleased.

"You know, if only you could teach me to be more like you, I am sure Mama would not be cross," mused Louisa-Margaretta. "She was once quite pleased that we were spending time together. Do you remember? And now she has lost hope that I shall turn out like you, and so she wishes to punish us both."

"Goodness," said Judith. "I am quite sure that is not it. Besides, have we not learned from each other? I am sure that I have been bolder thanks to your influence."

Louisa-Margaretta shook her head. There was something in her expression, an amusement that verged on anger, that Judith could not interpret. "I have not become more measured, though I ought to have changed. I may as well accept that I can never learn anything, that life will only grow worse by degrees from here to the end of my days."

Judith frowned at her friend's proclamation. "That seems rather morbid. And it isn't like you to be hopeless."

"Why shouldn't I be morbid and hopeless? Do you see that figure over there, walking off toward the stables?"

"Yes," said Judith patiently. "It is Mr Fletcher. You see him, too, every Sunday."

Thinking on it, she was not quite sure it was true. Mrs Haddington managed to convince her daughter to come to church some Sundays, but even her iron will did not prevail on a weekly basis. And when Louisa-Margaretta did attend, her inattention was obvious even to Judith's father, who was usually much more concerned about the content of his sermons than the minds of his parishioners. Though he cared deeply for his flock, he could not seem to understand why they would wish for short sermons and seemed impervious to the restlessness that ensued whenever he spoke at length.

"Mr Fletcher is the magistrate, remember?" asked Louisa-Margaretta. The man was not looking round, but she lowered her voice. "He seems quite sure that one of us killed the Duke."

Judith tried to suppress her natural feelings, but she could not fully repent of them. For a short period, the home where she had passed many of her happiest hours with Morgan and Louisa-Margaretta had been the site of a horrid attack. Her skin had turned cold every time she thought of the Duke, of what he'd wanted from her and what might have happened had they not been interrupted.

But since he was dead, the recollection no longer held the same power. What was more, why could she not go to Wycliff Castle? Though Papa had not said so, he had almost certainly been warning her about the Duke himself, and now that the man was dead, the place should be safe.

"I am sure Mr Fletcher will see reason, Louisa-Margaretta," Judith said. "He must know that nobody in your family would ever do such a thing."

"He seems more concerned about where we were, and in that respect, I may have a great deal of trouble convincing him of my innocence."

Judith could not help but laugh. "But you are innocent, Louisa-Margaretta! Really, he can hardly think otherwise just because you are odd enough to enjoy walking in such wicked weather."

"Wicked," murmured Louisa-Margaretta.

Judith sighed. "Well, then, I have not asked you what you think. How did the Duke come to die? And are the rumours true, that it must have been murder?"

Louisa-Margaretta nodded. "It was certainly murder. For he could not have hit himself in the head with a hammer or whatever it is. Nobody is quite sure who hit him or with what, but he could not have done it himself."

Judith shook her head. "Then I am sorry for him."

Louisa-Margaretta raised her eyebrows, and for a moment, Judith wondered if her friend knew more than she had revealed about what had befallen Judith that awful morning.

"You are sorry for him, Judith? Really? I would have thought such a man beneath your sympathy."

Judith blanched. "Nobody is supposed to be beneath my sympathy. As God forgives all sinners, so we must forgive others their trespasses."

"But you did not like the Duke and found many of his trespasses unforgivable."

Judith slowed her steps. No, she decided, it was not possible that Louisa-Margaretta knew precisely what the Duke had done to her. Surely, she would not tell such cruel jokes were she aware of exactly what sins could be laid at his door.

"It should be enough to say that I did not like him," said Judith, finality in her voice. "The question is 'Who did like him?'"

Louisa-Margaretta scowled. "His horrid friend Mr Galpin. Judith, I can tell you I believe that gentleman is worse than the Duke was. At least with the Duke, one could tell who he was, what he was thinking. Mr Galpin only sits about and smirks, and that is worse somehow."

"But there was real friendship between them?"

"I do not know that Mr Galpin could be a friend to anyone, not really. He is the only person I can think of who did not dislike the Duke. Both my parents hated him, though my father will not have said anything to anyone but Mama, and Mama would not consider murder to be a holy-enough solution."

"Oh, Louisa-Margaretta," said Judith, searching for Mr Fletcher. He must have gone into the stables, as she could no longer see him. "You ought not to speak of your mother that way."

Louisa-Margaretta took Judith's arm, leading her away from the house. "No, fine, but we know it was not my parents. That leaves Madame Chatel, her daughter, and the Duchess along with all the servants."

Judith frowned. "A woman? Would a smaller person have been able to kill the Duke in such a manner?"

"With the right sort of hammer, anyone can have a bash at the nearest bird-witted buffoon, Judith."

Judith knew that her expression was stern, but as it appeared to have no effect at all on her friend, she had to plead. "We cannot speak of him that way," she said. "He was a child of God, after all, who lost his life."

Louisa-Margaretta groaned. "You have admitted to hating him yourself, but fine. Those are the people who could have easily killed him. The only other possibility is that someone followed him all the way to Derbyshire, got into the castle without being noticed, and left without leaving a trace. And that is hardly a likely theory, although Mr Fletcher has asked about it. After all, it is the only thing that explains everything."

"How would that explain everything?"

"Well, both crimes, that is."

Judith stared. "Both crimes? Was there another besides killing the Duke?"

"Have you not heard? Perhaps it has not got about the village yet. The portrait that Madame Chatel was painting has been stolen."

33

———

Judith felt she had searched half the castle before a servant asked her what she was doing. She admitted that she was looking for Madame Chatel, and she was shown to the room where the woman stood, palette in hand, peering at a canvas.

Judith thought she hadn't been noticed, but the voice came across the room, clear and firm.

"Come bring me that cloth next to you, Miss St Clair. Since you have come for a social call, you may as well be useful." Madame Chatel spoke in French, in a clipped accent that Judith could not identify. Perhaps in times of distress, Madame Chatel spoke the French she had learned as a poor child playing in the Parisian streets.

Judith, shocked, grabbed the cloth and walked over to the painter. She expected that Madame Chatel would be working on a replacement for the painting that had been stolen, a new portrait of the Duke painted from memory. Instead, she found that the woman was doing a scene from life. It included the Haddingtons, their guests, and even Judith herself.

"This is all of us together." Judith frowned. "Madame, I am impressed that you remember every detail."

Judith herself had an excellent memory, and those around her often relied upon it. Her father had a good memory for Scripture, Louisa-Margaretta for verse, but Judith remembered most things about what she read and experienced. She did not have a perfect visual memory, though. While Madame Chatel might spend most of her time working on commissions for the wealthiest families of the *haut ton*, her gifts were certainly genuine.

"I did some sketches the other evening," said Madame Chatel, still not taking her eyes off her work. "You were all so distracted you probably hardly noticed the old woman."

Judith felt it as a rebuke. "I am sorry, Madame."

"No, you ought to enjoy each other's company in the evenings. My daughter is happier than I have seen her in some time, and I am sure it is thanks to these gatherings."

Judith frowned. Young Mademoiselle Chatel hardly seemed overcome with joy. In fact, except for the few conversations on the subject of roast goose at Michaelmas, the young woman had seemed almost despondent. Judith wondered just how out of spirits Mademoiselle Chatel must have been before if she now seemed genuinely happy.

"I hope we can provide some company for her, Madame," Judith said. "I did notice that she seemed rather quiet."

Madame Chatel snatched the cloth then threw it down next to her on a chair before gently setting the palette on top. "There is nothing wrong with my daughter," she said as if she had read Judith's thoughts.

"There is no shame in it," said Judith. "I was homesick when we first came here. I missed Essex every day and the village where I had spent most of my life." She had also missed her mother and still did, but she was not going to tell Madame Chatel. Something about the painter's brisk air did not invite confession.

"Why should she be homesick? I lived in Paris most of my life. Marie hardly knew it," Madame Chatel said, looking at the painting again and frowning.

"Perhaps that is the difficulty," said Judith. "Not having a sense of home must be rather trying."

"Yes, staying in castles as an honored guest, spellbound by the promise of roast goose," said Madame Chatel. "I often did not have enough to eat at her age, but she never thinks of that. Only of some fantasy."

Judith had known more than one woman like Madame Chatel. With a hard upbringing, in which she had not been permitted to fuss over things like the number of friends she had or her dreams for the future, Madame Chatel had grown strong. But the same strength also made her weak, for she was utterly unable to understand the feelings of her only daughter.

"It is difficult," she said gently, "but I admire the name you have made for yourself, Madame Chatel."

At that, the painter picked up her palette and brush and began working on part of the pianoforte. She had captured a moment when Louisa-Margaretta was sitting there, trying to play more quickly than she could manage so that Judith would have a moment to converse with Morgan. Though the painting was yet unfinished, Judith was alarmed to see that Madame Chatel had missed absolutely nothing. Judith and Morgan had stood near the piano, looking at one of the paintings on the wall, but she had captured the way they leaned toward each other, not touching but as close as etiquette would allow.

"It is nothing but hard work," said Madame Chatel.

However closely she had captured the moment that Judith and Morgan had shared, she was currently far too distracted to look at Judith and observe her blushes. "I had no choice but to apply myself, and so I did. Any woman could do the same."

"I am not terribly sure," said Judith, shifting from one foot to another. "I hope that I could, and yet I have little talent for painting."

"There are a thousand other things you could do," said Madame Chatel, choosing another color and working on Mrs Haddington's gown. "Painting is but one. I am sure you have thought of something before then dismissed it as not befitting a lady."

Judith gave a little smile. Madame Chatel was certainly perceptive, and with a start, she remembered how it was Morgan who had first laid out an idea for Louisa-Margaretta and Judith to sell their compositions. She thought about telling Madame Chatel that the two of them had written many songs together. Judith loved inventing the tunes, and Louisa-Margaretta was a genius with fitting words to them. Judith wrote everything out, taking pains to set the music down well, but they had never yet made any attempt to sell their work.

"It may be difficult for your daughter," Judith mused. "I never had to think about whether I would make a good clergyman, as I cannot become one. And so my father's successes never troubled me. But for Mademoiselle, depending as she does on your fortune and reputation, it must be troubling."

"My daughter is not troubled," snapped Madame Chatel.

Judith's eyes went wide. There was real venom in the

woman's voice, and she had once again set down her palette. She glared at Judith.

"Of course not," managed Judith. "I did not mean to say she was. I am so sorry." She was surprised she could manage any French as she quailed under the woman's stare.

"Miss St Clair," said Madame Chatel, surprising Judith. "I wish you would not come in with such implications. If you wish to make a living for yourself, you may as well get on with it."

Judith, shocked, stood there for a moment. Then an idea came to her.

"I am working on a very special piece of music," she said. "I have been writing it for some time, with Louisa-Margaretta's assistance. We mean to sell it when we are finished."

"Excellent," said Madame Chatel, although her tone was still sour. "Then you must share it with us very soon."

34

———

Louisa-Margaretta was sick of sitting with the Duchess. Every subject she tried to broach was met with a negative answer.

"Shall we play a game of Patience, perhaps?" she asked.

"I try to avoid playing cards" was the response. The Duchess was sitting so stiffly that Louisa-Margaretta wondered whether the woman was about to fall over.

"Perhaps we could write some poetry, then," she said. "I have my album, and the last thing I believe I put in it was a funny charade my mother had us make over the summer. She gets in these humours, you see, and wishes that we all write poetry about God and holidays and such. Even the rector does not make his daughters do it, but for Mama, it is as good as a prayer."

"Mm," said the Duchess with a little nod.

Louisa-Margaretta tried not to sigh. "Shall I bring the album?"

"I was taught that it was not proper for a lady to write poetry," said the Duchess, and Louisa-Margaretta gave a wan smile. She always wondered how other women accepted such nonsense about what a proper woman might and might not do. After all, were they not also aware that women owned banks, ruled empires, and rode into battle with men and indeed had done so for millennia? Even Louisa-Margaretta, who found history rather dull, enjoyed learning of women like Heloise. A lovely little religious lady, and yet she was burned up by lust and regret all the time and was so bold as to put her thoughts in writing!

But the Duchess must have felt nothing for such women, for she only sat stiffly, as if waiting for the next topic of conversation to emerge so she could take out the dagger of her ill humour and stab it to death.

Louisa-Margaretta went over to the pianoforte. After all, she had requested the Duchess accompany her to the Music Room not only because she found it pleasanter and less formal than many of the other rooms in Wycliff Castle but because she sincerely hoped the Duchess might speak more if they played together.

"Do you play or sing?" Louisa-Margaretta asked brightly. "I am afraid my friend Miss St Clair and I have been playing rather too much on this instrument, but I would dearly love to hear you perform."

For the first time, there was a small fluttering of interest. "I can play, if you would like," said the Duchess, sounding unsure.

"Yes," said Louisa-Margaretta firmly.

Judith still had some of her Bach set out, and the Duchess began to play it. Her playing was faithful but soulless. While Judith paid careful attention to tempo, the Duchess played as if each note were part of a military salute. There was no slowing when the feeling of the music required it, no speeding up to the sort of jaunty clip that was so natural to Judith. The way the Duchess played was completely flat. Louisa-Margaretta could hardly listen to it.

"That is wonderful," she said. "You play beautifully."

The Duchess stopped abruptly. "We always had to practice. Each day for half an hour."

Louisa-Margaretta blinked. "So little? And yet you play very well."

"It is all a matter of consistency," said the Duchess. "There was no time for more, but the master always stated that if we were to be faithful about playing every day, we would show great improvement over time."

"And so you have, I am sure," said Louisa-Margaretta. "He must have been very proud."

"My sisters were better," said the Duchess.

"Sisters! Goodness. I did not realise you had sisters. I have only brothers," said Louisa-Margaretta, seizing upon the subject. "Do any of your sisters live in England?"

"No," said the Duchess. "They married—well, their marriages were of a different sort."

The silence between them remained unbroken as Louisa-Margaretta contemplated the young woman's face. For the first time, the Duchess looked genuinely grieved rather than simply put out. For the duration of the visit, she and Judith had spoken of Mademoiselle Chatel as being most unfortunate in her homesickness. After all, that young woman had no home at all, and her only family members were an absent father and a rather neglectful mother. But the Duchess appeared just as lonely though perhaps more adept at hiding her feelings.

"Show me what you played with your sisters," said Louisa-Margaretta, inspiration coming to her as the Duchess frowned at her fingers.

And the woman began to play again, a strange and

mournful tune that Louisa-Margaretta had never heard. That time, though the young woman adhered to the tempo strictly, there was a hint of emotion in the music. Louisa-Margaretta suspected that nobody could play such a tune without any feeling. It had a darkness in it yet was clearly meant for dancing.

For a moment, Louisa-Margaretta's heart was captured by the music, then the Duchess stopped.

"That was beautiful," said Louisa-Margaretta.

The Duchess shook her head. "I have not played it in too long. I should not force you to listen to something I have not practised, a little folk song we used to play only for our own amusement. I apologise."

Louisa-Margaretta suppressed a sigh. Of course the young woman would apologise for the one thing she had done that was pleasant for her hosts. She unconsciously offended with most of her other words and actions, yet she offered no apologies for anything else. Did she not know that dismissing Louisa-Margaretta's every suggestion of activity as not befitting a lady was, in itself, exceptionally rude? For a moment, Louisa-Margaretta realised how out of her depth the woman must be in England, so strictly trained in the rules of etiquette without understanding their inherent purpose.

Even Louisa-Margaretta understood the purpose of society's strictures, little though she liked them. "They are all there so that you may avoid causing others discomfort and pain," Mama had always said. "That is why."

Louisa-Margaretta felt certain that the Duchess had never heard such an explanation but also wondered if she might exploit the young woman's naïveté to learn more about the murder. Though she herself considered it much more likely that Mr Galpin had murdered his friend, for some reason unknown to all of them, it suddenly occurred to her that the Duchess was the one who would most benefit from the man's death. With a large fortune at her fingertips, no children, and the respectability that her marriage had given her, she would have a degree of freedom that spinsters like Louisa-Margaretta could only envy.

"Will you visit your sisters soon?" she asked. "I am sorry. Perhaps you have not had the time to make any arrangements."

The Duchess's expression was closed once again. "I am not sure. I will not be able to travel for some time. Not while I am in mourning."

"I suppose not," said Louisa-Margaretta, though she disagreed. "Do you have all of the clothing you require? I hope Mama has offered you some of ours."

"Yes," said the Duchess, standing. "She has, but I have plenty of my own. I hope you will excuse me."

She left the room, leaving Louisa-Margaretta wondering why a young wife would travel with everything she needed for full mourning. When their family had gone into full mourning, even in their large and comfortable home, they had struggled to find all of the right dresses and cloaks. By the time they went into half mourning, they were prepared, and it was easier. If there had been a Haddington family death while the family was traveling, they certainly would not have had everything they needed.

And yet the Duchess's black dress fit her perfectly. Louisa-Margaretta had seen her in her black coat, and she had a mourning brooch that looked perfect for the occasion.

Did the young Prussian woman, with her cold expressions and her insistence on perfect manners, know she would soon be widowed?

35

Judith waited impatiently for her friend the next morning, and as soon as Louisa-Margaretta arrived, she insisted on visiting with her out of doors. She did not wish to attempt more than a brief walk, but they needed to share what they had learned the day before.

"Why did you rush away, Judith?" asked Louisa-Margaretta. "I have learned so many things, and I wished to speak with you."

"Because I ran into your mother," said Judith. "And I know it was terribly rude of me to come so soon. She plainly wished me gone, so I left."

"Well," said Louisa-Margaretta, "you ought to have courage and not let yourself be cowed by her the next time. For my cousin continues to pester me, and if you do not speak with him, I shall have no peace."

Judith looked away. She could have stayed with Mrs Haddington, had she really wanted to speak to Morgan, but she did not know what to say. It was easier to claim that she had visited Wycliff Castle without finding him then been forced to leave. She wanted to meet him while they had the safety of a large party around them. That way, they would not be forced to speak of the engagement, and she could simply enjoy his presence and draw strength from it.

"Tell me what you learned," said Judith abruptly. She did not wish to speak of Morgan, not even with her friend.

Louisa-Margaretta gave a sly smile. "First of all, the Duchess does not need any help with procuring the items she requires for deep mourning. She has everything with her in those ghastly trunks that she brought."

"She was well prepared," Judith said slowly.

"Exactly, and that is not reasonable. Also, she was evasive whenever I spoke of the thefts."

Judith shook her head. "Perhaps she is ashamed. It is a strange phenomenon, of course. Though I think I know how it might be done."

Louisa-Margaretta grabbed her arm. "You know? How on earth could you know?"

"I was in the room with Madame Chatel while she was painting," said Judith. "She did not seem to be paying a great deal of attention. And she often wants the windows open, even in winter. She claims that it makes subjects more ready to pose, as they are more awake, and it does something for the smell."

"Yes," said Louisa-Margaretta. "I hate the smell of paint."

Judith was amused for a moment. "And so all this sketching you have been doing? You are not about to make paintings from any of those?"

But Louisa-Margaretta did not laugh at the joke. She only shook her head. "I am done sketching," she said. "It was stupid of me. Go on about the windows."

"All right," said Judith. "So the windows are open, and sometimes, when Madame Chatel is working, she leaves the room. If someone is assisting her, she will ask that person to fetch things for her, but if not, I presume she must go herself or at least go to find a servant. I told her we could ring for someone, but she said that most of the servants would not be able to find the things that she needed."

Louisa-Margaretta nodded. "Well?"

Judith sighed. "I think it would be just possible to get a painting out of the window then pull it up to the room above."

Louisa-Margaretta laughed. "Oh, Judith, surely that is absurd!"

"But you could see," said Judith. "Will you look in the room and see if you can find the painting there?"

"No," said Louisa-Margaretta. "Come, Judith. Surely, no thief would leave it there! And I am not convinced that the thief is someone in our household."

"You think it is a stranger in our village, then? Who has arrived here completely undetected?"

"Perhaps," said Louisa-Margaretta, "you may wish to ask Mr Barnwell's opinion."

Judith sighed. It would be much more difficult for her to go wandering about in Wycliff Castle unremarked on than for Louisa-Margaretta to peek into the room in question. Judith couldn't remember which one it was. Wycliff Castle, even after all of the time she had spent there, was still a mystifying place.

"Whatever has Mr Barnwell to do with it?" asked Judith, her voice weary.

"Why, he is coming down the lane to see you," said Louisa-Margaretta, her voice full of mischief. "I think I should better leave the two of you alone."

"No," said Judith, but Mr Barnwell approached, and she forced herself to smile.

"Mr Barnwell!" said Louisa-Margaretta. "I must return to

my home this very instant. Perhaps you can walk the rest of the way back with Judith."

"Certainly," said the young man, offering his arm.

Judith could not think of a polite way to refuse, so she took his arm, all the while hoping that Morgan did not encounter them.

"Miss St Clair," said Mr Barnwell, "we are very near your home, and so I must be brief."

Judith stopped walking, letting go of Mr Barnwell's arm, but he kept her hand pressed in his.

"I-I am afraid you need not say anything more," she stammered.

She could not look directly at his face, but she sensed only surprise.

"Of course I must!" he said. "My dear Miss St Clair, I confess when I accepted employment with your father, I hadn't the smallest intention of finding a wife. But it is by the intercession of Providence that we have happened to share this sacred duty these months together. And I am sure that when we are married—"

Judith had to speak, though she could not find the words.

"I am very sorry, Mr Barnwell," she said. "I have absolutely no intention of marrying."

She extricated herself from his arm and, stumbling over her footsteps, apologised as she walked away.

"There is something I forgot to tell my friend! If you see my father, please let him know where I have gone."

36

In spite of all her anger at Louisa-Margaretta's jokes and schemes, Judith could speak of the proposal to no one else. She rushed to Wycliff Castle, almost by instinct, torn by her dislike of the place and her need to unburden herself to her dearest friend.

She was shown to a little sitting room, where she would wait until Louisa-Margaretta came to her. Judith always felt uneasy about those arrangements in Wycliff Castle. In all of the homes Judith had ever lived in or visited, any visitor could not help but find herself in the heart of the home after only a few steps. In the homes that were grand enough to have more than one sitting room where a family might assemble, still, the whole house would be small enough that she would know exactly where she was going and whom she would meet. But the first person to greet her was not Louisa-Margaretta—it was Morgan.

He was not announced, and Judith stood at the sight of him.

"Judith," he said. "I have narrowly escaped Madame Chatel. Now every time she sees me, she must have me as her opponent in a fiery debate. She cannot seem to understand that a united Europe is in everyone's interest, rather than the very specific revenge she wishes to exact on a certain set of revolutionaries. There is nothing I can say that does not provoke her."

He took several steps closer to Judith and held one hand in front of him. It looked as if he might take her hand and kiss it, but he stopped when he was not nearly close enough to do so. Perhaps the concern in her expression had stilled him.

"You should not be here," Judith said.

"Dost thou wish me gone?" he asked, the smile on his face underlaid by a certain gravity. But she loved the affection in the Quaker "thou" that he used and felt certain that it meant things were easier between them. Perhaps all of the darkness she had felt since their argument would be as nothing, a damp patch on a log that disappeared before the whole thing was consumed by fire.

She took comfort in the fire, watching the play of the flames. Wycliff Castle had its share of cold passageways, but whenever company was expected, all of the rooms used for entertaining were quite warm. It compensated, at least somewhat, for the expense of the furnishings, the sense that Judith always felt that if she broke any precious artifact, she would be too poor to ever replace it.

"Be easy, Judith," he said, taking another step toward her. His eye was on the open door. "My cousin will not be long."

Only a few paces lay between them, but Judith looked at the door. It would not be the first time that Morgan had kissed her, but it would be the first time in as many months, and she could not tell whether she longed more for the proof of his love or for the words that would bring her peace.

"We should not," she said without moving. "Imagine! Mrs Haddington hates me already."

"I am sure that is not true," said Morgan, but he did not sound certain. "At any rate, she does not hate *me*."

Judith tried to smile. She was still drawn to him but not at all certain that they would remain undiscovered.

"Truly, it is all right," he said. "After all, we are engaged."

Morgan, in his way, was only making the point that an engaged couple was often given rather more privacy than two young people known only to be in a serious friendship. But the mention of engagement made Judith catch her breath, and she sank again into her seat.

"I have offended you," he said. "I am sorry, Judith. I should not have assumed—"

"It is not that," she pleaded. "Only, Mr Barnwell asked me to marry him, just before I came."

"Mr Barnwell?" he asked. "That fellow who helps your father?"

"His curate, yes."

Morgan took not the seat next to Judith but the one beside that. All at once, rather than being caught in a compromising embrace, Mr Ramsbury and Miss St Clair would have appeared perfectly proper to anyone who happened upon them. That look of particular regard had fled from Morgan's face, the warm gaze that had only moments earlier marked Judith as the object of his affections.

"And you had no suspicion of his particular regard? I cannot believe you were completely surprised by this development."

Judith frowned. "Indeed, I was surprised. He is with

Papa so often, nearly a part of our family, that I had always supposed this to be the chief object of his visits."

"A part of the family, yes," said Morgan, and his voice twisted the words. "And your father wishes to make him a part of the family more formally. As do you."

"No," said Judith quickly. "You misunderstand me."

"I do not understand how you have gone so far as receiving a proposal from another young man while saying nothing of me to your family," said Morgan. "Nothing, not a word!"

"I can hardly choose what proposals I hear," hissed Judith. "Besides, I did not accept Mr Barnwell."

"And I suppose I am to be thankful for this?"

"I never asked you to be thankful." Judith's chest burned. "I came here to speak to Louisa-Margaretta, because even hearing Mr Barnwell speak in this manner grieved me. But I should not expect you to understand."

"Judith," he said, "I would understand, but I cannot. Thou must explain to me—"

"Nothing," she said, rising from her chair and making to leave the room. "I have done nothing dishonourable. I owe you no such explanation."

"Of course not! Judith, please."

She was at the doorway then. It would be terribly rude for her to rush off in her friend's home.

She was ready to be terribly rude.

"Stay," she hissed. "Tell your cousin Louisa-Margaretta I am gone. If you do not wish to offend me again, stay and do as I ask."

She could not be sure whether he had done it, as she rushed off. All she could do was hope that he would not follow her and that she could quickly find a room where she might weep in secret.

37

"Why did you come in here?" asked Louisa-Margaretta. "Nobody ever uses this room."

Judith looked away. "I wished to be alone for a moment," she said hastily. "And I forgot that this was the room above the one where Madame Chatel was working."

"Are you quite sure that he got the painting up here with ropes, though? It would have taken strength to pull it up through the window."

Judith nodded. "That is the best way to do it without being noticed. One could walk here, but without encountering a servant? It seems very unlikely."

Louisa-Margaretta touched her hair absently. There was something she had disliked about Mr Galpin from the beginning, but she could not imagine him as a thief. *Is he not a man of considerable means? And how could we know that he was selling the paintings for a profit?* It was very strange that anyone would pay for stolen portraits of the Duke. First of all, the Duke was not so close to the throne that the portraits would hold great value as depictions of a powerful ruler.

And second, most families of means would not be able to display such spoils publicly. Stolen jewels could be pried out of any necklace and put in a new setting—she knew that—but a portrait could not be disguised in that way.

Judith's cheeks were flushed. "We must go and speak with him. If he confesses, that will be the end of it."

"Whatever would possess you to say such a thing?" asked Louisa-Margaretta, laughing. "If he murdered his friend, do you really think we should speak to him together?"

"I do not see what else we can do," murmured Judith. "Oh, what does it matter?"

Louisa-Margaretta's eyes narrowed. "I am sure it does matter." She had been feeling very low since all of the trouble with Mr Chandler, but for the first time, she thought that Judith seemed even worse off. "Has something happened? Was my mother rude to you, or are you worried for Miriam?"

"Miriam spends all her time at the Chandlers', and your mama will not be troubled to speak with me," said Judith, her voice still soft.

Louisa-Margaretta almost jumped at the mention of the Chandlers, and she could feel her chest heaving as she struggled to stay ladylike and composed. After all, if someone were to join them in the room, they would have to look like nothing more than two friends having a peaceful chat.

"I am sorry," said Judith. The poor young woman apologised even in her deepest distress, and Louisa-Margaretta, who rarely attempted to make amends, found herself laughing again.

"I do not mean to say such things about your mother," said Judith. "Only, it has been the most terrible morning."

Louisa-Margaretta brightened. "No need to think of all that now. We shall go find my cousin then look for a murderer."

The jauntiness of her own voice cheered her, but Judith shook her head.

"Not your cousin," she said. "Please, not Morgan."

Louisa-Margaretta sighed. "True, I cannot think he would be much use in a fight. But there is a man here who would be."

Judith twisted her gown in her fingers. "A man here who can fight?"

"Yes," said Louisa-Margaretta. "Let us go and find my father."

38

———

Mr Haddington rarely said two words to Judith, but he was much more talkative on the subject of Mr Galpin than she had ever heard him.

"I will not," he said, and that was it.

"Papa," moaned Louisa-Margaretta. "Think of it. That awful Mr Fletcher is always here, running about and thinking that one of us hit the Duke over the head with a stick. And now, thanks to Judith, we know that Mr Galpin must have done so after stealing the portrait for some reason of his own."

Judith stood as far from Mr Haddington and Louisa-Margaretta as she could, examining some sketches that he had made of a prototype. His mind, she realised, would ever be that of a creator. If he could think of a machine that might be helpful, he would build it. And he would not be best pleased if it were destroyed, she knew, thinking back to the dark looks he gave anyone who spoke of the Luddites.

"We only need to speak to him, to start," said Judith. "Then we can tell the magistrate."

"Neither of you will do such a thing," said Mr Hadding-ton. "It is not worth the risk, and I'll hear no more of it."

He looked so uncommonly stubborn that Judith felt ready to give up. Louisa-Margaretta, of course, would press him.

"We can all speak to him about something else, then," she said. "We will talk of art in general or the fashions in London or some other silly thing. But you would not like Judith and me going about unaccompanied, would you?"

"No," he said. After a long stare from Louisa-Margaretta, he spoke. "Well, Lou. I will stay with both of you while we send for the magistrate. If that Mr Galpin is still about, we ought to be together."

"Thank you, Papa," said Louisa-Margaretta, her expression equal parts satisfaction and sweetness. Judith suspected it was an expression she often wore around her father, who seemed always to be bent to the will of the imperious young woman.

But Judith, who had been listening to the conversation without doing battle, heard what her friend did not. "If he is still about?" she asked. "Mr Galpin is gone?"

39

They sent for the magistrate. According to Mr Haddington, Mr Galpin had already been gone for the better part of the day. And they had no definite knowledge as to his whereabouts. He had been in the village, but in spite of all the gossip, nobody could say for certain where he had ended up after that.

Louisa-Margaretta made sure that Mr Fletcher spoke to members of the family in the Antelibrary, as it had once been part of the Cabinet Library. The wall that separated the two rooms was rather thin.

"I'm sure we ought never to do this," Judith whispered, frowning at her friend as they stood with their ears to the wall. "There may be some kind of a law against it."

"There is no such thing," said Louisa-Margaretta, then she lowered her voice when she remembered that those on the other side of the wall might hear. "Don't be silly. And we shall never have the slightest idea what is going on unless we know what that horrible man is thinking."

"I am not so sure that Mr Fletcher is horrible," said Judith. "His suspicions have been well-reasoned, if false.

After all, how is he to feel certain about the character of anyone here? If nothing else, he has probably heard all manner of rumours about the misfortunes that have come before this one."

"Then he is a most unreasonable fool," Louisa-Margaretta said firmly. "And if you join me here, you will be able to hear much more. You are standing right where there is a fireplace opposite. You will hear nothing."

Judith hesitated, unwilling to move from her place. Louisa-Margaretta returned her ear to the wall. She had discovered that she needed to stand very close to the wall, with her ear not quite touching it, in order to hear the conversation in the other room.

At first, it was not much of a conversation. Mr Fletcher was speaking to Mr Haddington, but the latter made such small answers that Louisa-Margaretta understood why others thought Papa rather weak and insipid. That had always been one of his strengths in business, she knew. He seemed a bit thick and too shy to do any real harm. His enemies were wrong in those assumptions, but they often realised their mistake too late.

"I had some questions about your nephew," Mr Fletcher said.

There was a murmured response, then the magistrate went on.

"Yes, a relation of your wife's, I understand. He has claimed to be working at the Inns, and he will become a solicitor."

Another murmur. *Oh, Papa!* Louisa-Margaretta knew that he would not be speaking louder unless sorely provoked, so she could only guess at his responses to the rude interrogation.

"He has left too late to return to the Inns by Michelmas, now that we have asked everyone to remain at Wycliff Castle," said Mr Fletcher. "It is a very curious time for him to be visiting. What did he claim his purpose was in coming to your family during this visit, making work for you when you are so busy?"

Papa said something that Louisa-Margaretta knew must have been, "We welcome guests." It was usually said to Louisa-Margaretta herself, in a shaming fashion, when Mama felt that she was not offering sufficient hospitality. Mama would go on about God's wishes, social graces, and what wifely expectations she must meet in the future, but Papa's three-word admonishment was much more efficient. If he said it in a firm voice, there was a slight chance that Louisa-Margaretta would listen.

She knew her guess had been right, but it was not much consolation when she heard what else Mr Fletcher had to say. Louisa-Margaretta had to drag her friend over by her arm so that Judith could hear all of the man's speculations. *Gracious, poor Judith. She must never eat.* Her body felt both light and weak as Louisa-Margaretta steered it to the correct corner.

"I understand the young man has been speaking out quite a bit, offending his guests, stating that Bonaparte and the likes of him must be allowed to continue on in France," said Mr Fletcher. "I wonder what the Duke thought of these sentiments."

More murmuring. The answer must have made no difference to Mr Fletcher.

"Make no mistake," he said. "I am interested in the whereabouts of your Mr Galpin, yes, particularly as we cannot seem to learn how he left the village, and he cannot have got far in this weather. But I think he may be protecting himself from a dangerous element you have under your roof, sir, and in your own family."

Louisa-Margaretta looked at her friend. Judith was pale. But instead of fainting, she seemed stronger.

"We must warn Morgan," Judith said.

Louisa-Margaretta shook her head. Papa was speaking, but it seemed Mr Fletcher was finished for the moment.

"What good would that do?" Louisa-Margaretta whispered. "Mr Fletcher has made up his mind."

"All the more reason we must change it," said Judith. "Imagine! And it is all my own fault. If I had simply spoken with my family, he would not have come at all, and none of this would have happened."

Her thin frame suddenly steely, she was out the door before Louisa-Margaretta could try to change her mind.

Louisa-Margaretta frowned. She would go back up and get the portrait, she decided. If there was a chance anyone could cast more suspicion on Mr Galpin, perhaps her cousin would be spared. Perhaps he rather deserved it, going on as he did about monarchies and revolutions, but anyone who mistook Cousin Morgan's political ramblings for some kind of violent plan of attack must be a simpleton. And for Judith's sake, she would need to prove it.

40

Judith had not imagined that she would speak with Morgan soon. She was still wounded by his attack, angry with him, and above all, regretful that their engagement might not continue. Since her mother's death, it was Morgan and Louisa-Margaretta who had brought meaning to her days, and it seemed impossible that she could lose one of them forever due to her own cowardice.

And even if she did lose Morgan, she was resolved not to let him go to the scaffold for her. Perhaps they would not marry, but she would report all of the details of their secret engagement faithfully in order to save his life. *Would things be so much worse?* She would surely not be disowned by her family if she thought the better of things and married Mr Barnwell, and then at least Morgan would live.

But when she found him, after hurrying out to the grounds in pursuit, he had very little interest in Mr Fletcher.

"Judith," he said. "I must apologise again. Only, I have been half mad, wondering if we can marry, and it has driven me to all sorts of terrible lengths. Please forgive me."

He held his gloved hands in front of him, his whole face clouded by worry. But Judith could not make him easy.

"I am so sorry," she said. "I do not know whether we will marry, honestly, Mr Ramsbury. But I came to warn you."

He was hurt by her address. That was plain. They had been "Morgan" and "Judith" to each other since the early days of their courtship, when they had stood in those same beautiful grounds in the spring, and Judith could feel every single thing she loved about both humans and the natural world returning to her at once, fastening into her soul perfectly.

"Warn me, then," he said, frowning at her. He looked more confused than concerned.

"You must listen," Judith said. "Mr Fletcher came here asking about your visit. He believes that it is suspicious that you are not at the Inns and seems to think that you came because you hate men like the Duke."

"What?" Morgan began to smile. "Then he is more foolish than I thought. Besides, he expressly forbids me from returning to the Inns until this whole matter is resolved, so for all he knows, I stay here at his pleasure."

"Yes, but it is a strange time of year for you to visit, especially when the family had such important visitors, and Mr Fletcher has made no discoveries as to the real perpetrators of this crime," said Judith. "It seems very much as if he is settling on you."

Morgan held up his hands. "What can I say? I didn't kill the Duke."

"Of course not." Judith nearly cried in frustration. "But if he thinks you did, I must tell him of the reason for your visit. I will tell him of our engagement."

"You will do no such thing," said Morgan. "And I release

you from such a mad idea by telling you this. If you do say something to Mr Fletcher, I will deny it all."

Judith stared at him. "You would not."

"I would," he said, and Judith thought she had never heard words so cruel in her life. She could only respond to them by turning away, heading toward Wycliff Castle and her friend.

41

Louisa-Margaretta had examined the little room all she could, but she was no closer to finding proof of Mr Galpin's crime. The trouble with him was that he pretended he had all the answers. Then when answers were needed, he absconded. She wondered where on earth the man could be so well concealed. He had money, to be certain, but was it really enough to bribe one of the residents of the village into harbouring a fugitive?

Judith rushed in, cap askew.

"Oh." She sat down in the nearest chair then became very still.

"Did you warn my cousin?" asked Louisa-Margaretta. "I hope he told you it would not be wise to reveal your secret engagement to the whole world in this manner. Perhaps wait until neither of you is accused of murder."

Judith shook her head. "There is no engagement," she said, her voice distant.

Louisa-Margaretta walked over and sat next to her friend. "You must be mad. No engagement? He broke it off because you warned him about that silly Mr Fletcher?"

Judith nodded.

Louisa-Margaretta gave an exasperated sigh. "There we have it. He is just as much a ninny as the next man. I suppose we ought not to have expected more of him. That was the trouble."

Judith put a hand to her forehead. Louisa-Margaretta knew her friend well enough to realise that Judith would try not to weep, would put all her strength into making herself appear well. It was a silly endeavor, in Louisa-Margaretta's mind. Better to wail as loudly as possible and then feel angry. That way, all the troubling feelings would be out sooner. But she knew well that she could not rush Judith.

"Very well," she said. "Cousin Morgan is a stupid man. But he is not vicious. I am sure, in an act of noble sacrifice, you wish to prove that he did not kill the Duke?"

Another nod.

"We shall have to concentrate on those guests that are left, before one of them disappears," said Louisa-Margaretta, getting to her feet. She reached down to grab one of her friend's hands. "Very well, Judith. You may pity yourself later, once our work is done. I am going to speak to the Duchess. I will rely on you to speak to that horrid Madame Chatel. You need not gather yourself much at all. She will only wish for an audience."

At that, Judith stood. "Thank you," she said, her voice weak.

"Nonsense," said Louisa-Margaretta. "I am cross with Cousin Morgan, but at any rate, I shall help him. And you can tell me later how very kind and noble I have been. I shall expect a great deal of praise."

42

J udith found Madame Chatel engaged in conversation with Mrs Haddington. She almost made her apologies and left, but she recalled the need to get information about someone other than Cousin Morgan. And Madame Chatel had lived through a great deal of difficulties. She was never precisely open about what had made her leave France, stating only that her first two attempts to escape Paris had not worked, and for her young daughter's sake, she had been willing to go through any amount of danger to escape the city.

Did she steal? Or perhaps even kill someone? It seemed unlikely, but there was a hardness to her. Madame Chatel had said on more than one occasion that she did what she had to do to survive. Also, her husband had left Paris first, and it was unclear what had become of him. Perhaps the grand painter was in the habit of murdering men whose presence was inconvenient.

Judith had an example of the painter's coldness as soon as Mrs Haddington started to speak on the subject of her husband's business.

"It usually occupies him a great deal," said Mrs Haddington. "He has needed to get to Manchester for some days now, but he must conduct all his business from afar because of Mr Fletcher."

"That is his business," said Madame Chatel. "What of yours?"

"I keep this house," said Mrs Haddington, "and I see to our tenants who are in need as well as to the children. That is my business."

Madame Chatel shook her head. "Your children are grown. You might go into business yourself, Madame. It is safer that way."

Mrs Haddington smiled. "I am quite happy not to. I was raised to expect running a household to occupy my hours, and so it does."

"Your daughter? What means does she have?"

Judith's eyes flitted from one woman to the other. She thought it abominably rude for Madame Chatel to ask such questions. Then again, Mrs Haddington was often so direct in her own manner as to be considered rude, and she did not seem to mind the inquisition.

"Her father will settle a most generous sum on her when she marries," said Mrs Haddington. "Her fortune was to be twenty thousand pounds. Alas, since our Louisa-Margaretta has not wished to marry yet, her father and I wish to make it thirty thousand pounds. That way, there will always be money for her, should she be in need of it."

Judith tried not to nod. The purpose often given for settling a great sum on a daughter was that the daughter might need to have money of her own, were she to be widowed. But with Louisa-Margaretta, the purpose was to guard against future folly. Judith knew that after a secret engagement to a man her family considered unsuitable, a dangerous flirtation with Mr Fortescue, then an extended period of time without a decent offer, Louisa-Margaretta was becoming ever less attractive as a prospect. Even fortune hunters could find an easier mark. She had thought Mrs Haddington ignorant of much of that, at least the bit about Mr Fortescue, but perhaps her friend's mother knew more than she was saying. If so, it was little wonder that she blamed Judith for Louisa-Margaretta's unfortunate dalliance with that gentleman. Judith had been closest to Louisa-Margaretta when Mr Fortescue was making his first advances, and though she had hated the man on sight, perhaps Mrs Haddington suspected her of somehow encouraging the illicit attachment.

"That young man was saying something about selling music," said Madame Chatel. "Mademoiselle St Clair, is that not correct? The troublesome Monsieur Ramsbury believes that you and your friend ought to sell your compositions."

Mrs Haddington frowned, and Judith felt most uneasy. Morgan had said for some time that the songs she and Louisa-Margaretta came up with were good enough to sell, but Judith knew nothing of such transactions, and she had always assumed that both their families would disapprove. The most she had done was to write them all down neatly, so that she and Louisa-Margaretta would not forget anything. Even that had been a rather silly exercise, as Judith herself could remember all the songs easily. But she had found that drawing the neat lines and the elegant notes had been a pleasing exercise.

Still, she hoped that Mrs Haddington was quite ignorant of their efforts.

"We compose these little ditties for our own amusement, nothing more," Judith said, trying to warn Madame Chatel off the subject.

"Nonsense. They are very clever. And then you see, neither of you would depend on the goodwill of a father or brother for your livelihood."

Judith shifted in her seat, and Mrs Haddington took over. "Both young ladies are fortunate to have truly excellent brothers. Neither would ever be allowed to want for a thing, I assure you."

Judith had many responses to that. She knew that she might, indeed, be able to "want for" many things in the future. The Haddingtons' patronage had allowed her father to claim the most lucrative position of his lifetime, but Judith knew it could disappear at any moment.

And for that reason, she knew that she needed to win back Mrs Haddington's goodwill. "Indeed," she said quietly. "Madame Chatel, do you have any other subjects to paint during your stay here? I hope you will allow me to assist you again."

The painter threw her a contemptuous glance. "It doesn't do to talk of independent young women. Is that it? You English are always turning the conversation to something else when I suggest it. Ah, Mademoiselle St Clair, I shall answer you. Yes, I would very much like to paint someone else. And Monsieur Haddington, do you think he would sit for me?"

Mrs Haddington gave a wide smile. "He is tired of being held up here, but I am sure he will. Though as a rule, he does not like having his portrait done."

Madame Chatel smiled. "Ah, it would be a joy to paint him! Those figures with hidden depths are the most interesting."

Mrs Haddington shook her head, a pained smile on her face. "I am sure he would not like that description, Madame Chatel. He has nothing hidden."

"Some may think his features weak," said Madame Chatel.

Judith, who felt that her features were rather weak in comparison with the statuesque Louisa-Margaretta or the exceedingly pretty Miriam, frowned, but Madame Chatel went on to compliment Mr Haddington.

"His face is changeable," she said, "every expression written on it, though he is a reticent one, eh? That is gold for a painter. It is a pity his hair is so thin, though not uncommon in a man of his age."

"Yes, well." Mrs Haddington clasped her hands and smiled widely.

Judith thought something in her smile seemed forced. Perhaps she foresaw the work of needing to speak with her husband, to convince him to sit for the demanding woman. "He may sit for you. I am very happy to ask him."

Madame Chatel smiled. "Good. For if I have no work, and he has almost nothing to do outside of Manchester, we shall both end up in the madhouse! Work is all that is needed for one's spirits in a time like this. It shall all come right."

"We need not speak of the madhouse," said Judith, quickly blushing. She wondered if Mrs Haddington would be more aggravated at the reminder of the sorry state Louisa-Margaretta had been in when they returned to Derbyshire. Perhaps, Judith hoped, Louisa-Margaretta's mama would simply be glad that someone else was standing in the way of Madame Chatel's grand pronouncements.

"Indeed not," said Madame Chatel. "Not when there is work to be done."

Judith stood up, ready to assist the painter, and Mrs Haddington rang for a servant to help them.

Perhaps, Judith thought, the work would take her mind

off Morgan. For all Madame Chatel's talk, Judith had learned nothing new about the murder. She only hoped that the grand distraction of painting would loosen Madame Chatel's tongue. For something about the woman's convictions concerning men made Judith uneasy. Though many women spoke of the importance of independence for their daughters, it was always, in the manner of Mrs Haddington, as an unfortunate necessity, not an aim in and of itself. Independence was something that might befall a young woman were her husband to die. In fact, the Duchess was going to be quite independent.

Judith wondered if Louisa-Margaretta might ascertain the Duchess's feelings on the matter and whether that independence was a sudden surprise or a motive for murder.

43

L ouisa-Margaretta's resolve to try her best with the Duchess began to fail as soon as she turned the conversation to the future.

"Will you go back to Prussia?" she asked.

The Duchess's look was so polite it was almost blank. "Pardon me, Miss Haddington?"

"Perhaps you do not know your plans," said Louisa-Margaretta. "I only thought you might not wish to stay in England! But if you did not, Prussia would not be the only place you could live."

"Quite," said the Duchess.

Louisa-Margaretta's toes curled in frustration. If the Duchess had murdered her husband, it was clear that she was never going to come close to admitting it.

"I mean," Louisa-Margaretta reasoned, "I am sure that I do not wish to be like Madame Chatel, always telling others how they ought to live their lives."

The Duchess gave a sad smile, a faint light coming into her eyes for the first time. "I spent the first part of my life being told exactly how to be a lady. Then the rest of it was spent fulfilling those lessons. I suppose I do not find Madame Chatel's manner objectionable for that reason."

Louisa-Margaretta, who had hoped the woman would finally start talking, fumbled for an answer. "Learning how to be a lady?"

"Yes," said the Duchess. "Learning how never to object to anything that happens within the family's gates. It was a lesson I never learned fully, perhaps."

"You did not?" breathed Louisa-Margaretta.

"When one cannot raise objections with words, one will find another manner," said the Duchess.

Louisa-Margaretta was thrilled. Her strange little complaints about Madame Chatel had goaded the woman into a confession! What a wonderful reward for her efforts. She nearly held her breath, nodding.

"Another manner?" she asked.

The Duchess, however, had gone back into the state of being that was more familiar to her. She was a lady once again, answering each question with one or two polite words. She had learned how to do that, and yet it seemed she had never learned how to have any openness or sincerity in a conversation. That was why it was so unpleasant to spend time with her, Louisa-Margaretta realised. Though every polite lady might complain, at times, at having to keep to certain subjects, the rules of politesse did not demand that they relinquish every genuine feeling. The Duchess had been taught to be so "polite" that her responses were wooden, soulless.

"I would not know so much about that," Louisa-Margaretta said. "I have never been married, though of course my parents wish it for me."

She thought that might bring some response, but the Duchess was nearly motionless again. "Yes, it is beneficial."

"But what about after the marriage happens?" asked Louisa-Margaretta, trying to draw out that flash of spirit she had briefly seen in the other woman. "I fear that I may learn certain things only when it is too late."

The Duchess hardly looked at her. "A marriage is a blessing," she said, and her voice was so gentle that Louisa-Margaretta would almost have thought that she meant it.

Louisa-Margaretta grew angry. But she could not help thinking about that piece of advice as a balm for her own sorry situation. Instead of running about, fearing the consequences of her actions, she could simply get married. If she had been married in the first place, even what had happened with Mr Chandler would have caused no great scandal. Married women were not exactly allowed to do as they liked, but with the right amount of discretion, they might be forgiven many mistakes. Such a dalliance would sink the reputation of a spinster, but it might be overlooked in an otherwise respectable matron.

"I'm sorry," Louisa-Margaretta said briskly. "You were perfectly right. An advantageous marriage is a solution to many ills. And in many cases, it is advantageous for both parties, making it a very happy event indeed."

She stood unsteadily. She hated her body for its weakness, for what she saw as its betrayal. When she was quite young, she thought she would be married as a matter of course. Then, when she met Isaac, it seemed certain. After losing him, she was determined to stay a spinster.

Once more, her fortunes had changed. She needed to marry, and if the banns were read tomorrow, it would not be too soon. Though the Duchess said little enough, on that point, she was absolutely correct.

A marriage, in Louisa-Margaretta's case, would be a blessing indeed.

44

Mr Barnwell was downstairs, paying a call on her mother. That, Louisa-Margaretta learned from a housemaid, and it was all she needed to know.

She would propose marriage to him. The Duchess had been utterly dependent on her husband. And Louisa-Margaretta knew that, much as she would like to avoid such a fate, she could not afford to be particular. Mr Barnwell wanted a wife, and having a respectable young curate as her husband would solve at least some of her problems.

Like the problem of her fluttering heart, the new heaviness in her brow. Louisa-Margaretta was not so naive as to be unaware of the physical changes that a certain condition brought about, and she knew she would need to act quickly. It would be a matter of deceiving Mr Barnwell, of course, but she could be forgiven as soon as they were married.

For a moment, her heart whispered that Mr Barnwell had wanted to marry Judith. But that was no great obstacle for Louisa-Margaretta. After all, she knew very well that she was much handsomer than her friend, and she had a fortune that would set her husband up quite comfortably. Louisa-Margaretta herself would rather have more than her dowry and a curate's meagre pay to live on, but for him, it would be a paradise of riches.

She was fortunate. Her mother had not yet entered the room.

"Mr Barnwell," she said, "thank you for calling on us."

"I came to see your mother," he said. "But it is a pleasure to see you here as well, Miss Haddington."

That was all the invitation Louisa-Margaretta needed. She swept over to where Mr Barnwell had stood, sat down, and invited him to do the same.

"I understand that you wish to marry," she said. "And that my friend Miss St Clair does not."

He looked pale then angry. "I hardly thought—"

"Oh, don't trouble yourself," she said, reminded again why she had never found the man easy to like. "Judith is no gossip. But you can hardly hope to spring a surprise offer of marriage on a young lady then ask her to keep it from her dearest friend. That would be cruel indeed."

He made no answer, though his expression was grim.

"I came to tell you that I am ready to marry," she said. "To be quite honest, I would like to settle here. And so, I am sure you would never think of asking me, due to our relative positions. But you will ask, and I shall accept you."

"What on earth do you mean?" he asked.

"My parents will settle thirty thousand pounds on me," Louisa-Margaretta went on. "So you can go on being a clergyman, if you wish it, but you needn't do it if you would prefer not to."

Seeing that Mr Barnwell had fallen silent, she frowned at him. "Well?"

"Am I supposed to be flattered by your offer?" he asked.

"I declared my affection for your friend, as you apparently know. You seem to think I am the sort of fellow who will forget his feelings in the face of an enormous sum of money. I am not sure if I ought to be insulted or flattered that you wish to marry me in spite of that rather bleak judgement of my character."

Louisa-Margaretta would have been happy to chastise him, but her mother came to find her first.

"Madame Chatel is going to paint your father," she told Louisa-Margaretta. "Mr Barnwell, I am so sorry to have kept you waiting! Come, sit down."

Louisa-Margaretta did not wait to hear what the idiotic curate would say. She had only just resigned herself to marrying him, and all at once, he was ready to reject her! The fact that she had named the exact sum of her dowry made the sting even greater. It was impossible to pretend that Mr Barnwell was ignorant of any of the particulars, yet still, he did not wish to marry.

Madame Chatel had her sketching things, but she was working on a still life.

"Thank you for coming, Miss Haddington," she said. "Your father does not wish to sit for me just yet. I would like to hear more about this scheme of selling music with your friend Miss St Clair. It seems a very wise way to ensure that you need not depend on your brothers or even on your parents."

"Really?" said Louisa-Margaretta. "I think it is an abominable idea and a very easy way for us to introduce privation into our lives. And if we are not allowed to put our own names to the music, what is the purpose?"

She could see that her complaints were not received gently.

"You can put your own name to your music," said

Madame Chatel. "I do not understand how you English gentlewomen accept such things. Nobody paints. Nobody feels it is elegant to earn even a single shilling! Perhaps if my daughter and I had been English, with such a father as she has, we would have starved."

"You would not starve here," Louisa-Margaretta snapped. "In case you were wondering, we have a regent on the throne, and our government is quite intact."

Her words did not sting, though she had hoped they would. Instead, Madame Chatel looked thoughtful. "For all you English say about France, Mademoiselle, you are correct on that point," she said. "But I would much prefer a country where what happened in France is seen for the tragedy that it was, and in spite of your stability, you cannot boast of that here. Young men like your cousin like to drink to what they claim are principles, all on the graves of my friends."

Louisa-Margaretta scowled. "My cousin hardly drinks. And I'm sure he does not mean to dance on any graves."

Madame Chatel still shook her head. "It is of no consequence. At any rate, Mademoiselle, you will make your own decisions about your livelihood. But in service of mine, I need you to bring me that painting of the Duke. I must finish it so it is ready to sell."

Louisa-Margaretta stared at her. "You would not sell it!"

Madame Chatel gave her a sharp look. "Of course I shall sell it! Do not pretend to be ignorant of my circumstances. My daughter and I must provide for ourselves, especially if we are to journey to a place where we do not have to entertain the likes of your cousin. And considering the event, the portrait will fetch a handsome sum indeed."

A new idea occurred to Louisa-Margaretta, covering her

features with suspicion. "Is that why the Duke had to perish?"

Madame Chatel got close to Louisa-Margaretta. "Mademoiselle, how dare you! I have spent my days here trying to convince the likes of your family that murder is never acceptable and especially not for a so-called cause. And you think I would kill a man for profit! You rich families, you have no idea what you are about."

Louisa-Margaretta was silenced by the rebuke. She had found all of Madame Chatel's tirades tedious, and yet thinking of her own life, for a moment, they seemed understandable. If some war or movement had resulted in the death of one of her brothers or Judith or her parents, she was sure that she would never have accepted any of it as just. She was as hot-blooded as Madame Chatel, but because she had never been tested, she could pass herself off as reasonable if not demure more of the time.

"Very well, Madame," said Louisa-Margaretta. "I shall bring you the painting, and I hope you get a very good price."

45

Louisa-Margaretta marched down the cold passage, feeling a grudging sense of respect for the old lady and her paintings. If Louisa-Margaretta was not going to leave Wycliff Castle under happy circumstances herself, she could at least do one thing for their illustrious guest. She was rather ashamed that she had believed that Madame Chatel disliked her. What the painter disliked, she could see, was the sight of a young woman of ability unable to earn her keep.

Louisa-Margaretta tried to consider things from Madame Chatel's lofty perspective. Perhaps she could start selling music with Judith. Thanks to Judith's diligence, many of the songs they had written were already put to paper. And even when visitors did bring gifts of music to Louisa-Margaretta, she was often surprised by the poor quality. Judith could write better tunes, and she could certainly write words that were more humorous and more poignant.

But it was no use. Louisa-Margaretta's mind raced, her body heavy with the unfamiliar sensations of fatigue and defeat. She would find that painting and let Judith solve the murder. When it was all sorted, Louisa-Margaretta would find a man to marry her. There probably was no man who would take her in that condition, apart from Mr Fortescue. She would get exactly what she deserved.

The State Music Room was dark. Louisa-Margaretta knew that it had to be kept dark and cold to preserve the furniture, but the smell was ghastly. She was reminded instantly why she avoided the place. It was going to be difficult to find even the portrait of the Duke without a candle. Instead of going to the trouble, Louisa-Margaretta let her eyes adjust then moved around an old settee covered with a cloth. Whoever had taken the painting there would not have put it far. She knew that many of the servants, though they did not have the luxury of disobedience, were nevertheless so superstitious that they would not have even wanted to touch the thing. Harriet had told her as much.

She saw some shape, under a cloth, that must have been a painting. She bent down to touch a corner of the cloth, and drawing it up, she found herself face-to-face with a large bust of Homer.

"Stop," a voice said, and Louisa-Margaretta was still with shock.

46

Judith wanted to see the music that she had composed with Louisa-Margaretta. Madame Chatel had been ordering her to sell it and to convince her friend to join her in creating a true partnership. Judith, who did not have any business connections or the legitimacy of a well-known family, would likely have difficulty putting her work before any stranger. She needed Louisa-Margaretta, but her friend had accepted defeat before they had even begun.

When they had first spoken of it, Louisa-Margaretta had been against the scheme.

"Madame Chatel thinks we all must be geniuses, like she is," Louisa-Margaretta had grumbled. "It does not strike her as possible that a young woman could ever be trapped, she has had such a lucky escape herself."

"Madame Chatel would say that geniuses are not born but made by the paint on their fingers," Judith mused.

"That is a very stupid way to phrase it," said Louisa-Margaretta. "Oh, Judith, don't take offense. You know that Madame Chatel is hardly right in the head."

"Do I?" asked Judith. "She is the first woman painter I have ever met, and I must confess that her commissions have impressed me."

Louisa-Margaretta could not listen. "She is an arrogant old taskmaster, and she knows nothing of our future. She is so in love with her own pronouncements she cannot help attempting to make everyone around her rich."

"You are already rich," said Judith.

As she crept about the room, remembering that conversation, Judith came to a decision.

She did not think she would be rich, but she wished for just a little of the security that Louisa-Margaretta had. After all, one compelling reason for her to accept Mr Barnwell was that she would eventually be the burden of one of her brothers. Apart from her father's living, and the money they had carefully put away in the years after their move to Derbyshire, her family had very little. Even a single jewel from one of the necklaces that Louisa-Margaretta habitually wore would give Judith enough to live on for years, if she lived on her own with the utmost frugality. If they were not great successes in their music scheme but made enough for her to have at least some savings, she might be able to make the argument for continuing as a spinster rather than tying herself to someone like Mr Barnwell.

To accomplish that, she would need to gather the music then find a way to correspond with some individual in London who could help them. If Louisa-Margaretta would not help, perhaps Madame Chatel had a friend who would give Judith an address. Though she tried not to let herself depend on the scheme, by the time she got to the room where they had stored everything they had completed, the flame of hope was growing brighter. Louisa-Margaretta wanted money of her own, and in spite of her stubborn character and love of sleep, she had proved to Judith that she was capable of working hard when her position demanded it. Judith would be a fool to think that they were doomed to fail in their endeavors.

She found the music next to a bust of Homer. But just then, she heard footsteps, and she knew Wycliff Castle well enough to tell that there was no good reason for anyone to come to that wing. The amount of dust in the room made it clear that even the servants avoided it.

Creeping behind some odd piece of furniture, Judith clutched the bust, her heart racing. She had never been strong, never been any good at defending herself. But since meeting Louisa-Margaretta, she had been in many terrifying situations. If she had learned anything, it was to think through her response as carefully as she could and never admit defeat. Even a murderer might well be thrown off guard by a bold, prepared young woman.

The footsteps were closer. Taking a deep breath, Judith raised the bust over her head then stepped out. "Stop!"

"Judith?" came the response. "Put that bloody thing down. You'll kill me!"

Judith would have been more shocked at Louisa-Margaretta's coarse language had she not been concentrating on the bust, by then very close to Louisa-Margaretta's silky hair. Judith lowered the heavy sculpture slowly, breathing gently.

"Louisa-Margaretta," she said. "I am so sorry. I did not think—"

"Did Madame Chatel send you up here too?" Louisa-Margaretta smoothed her beautiful hair, already recovering herself. "That woman and her precious portrait. I know it will fetch a good sum, but truly, the way she has decided to exploit the Duke's death is rather ghastly."

"I could have killed you," Judith said slowly.

"Best not to dwell on it, Judith. I daresay we have other concerns at the moment. Now put that thing down. I'll take the painting, and then we can go have tea and forget the inglorious Madame Chatel for an afternoon."

"No, Louisa-Margaretta," said Judith. "What I am trying to tell you is that we have not considered the Duke's actions. What if he was the attacker and his murder only a defense as natural as the one that I attempted just now?"

Louisa-Margaretta tossed her head from side to side, grabbing the painting and lifting it easily. "That hardly seems likely. And what would that mean? That he was fighting with some man? Another duel?"

"No," said Judith. "The opposite. His killer must have been a woman."

47

J udith and Louisa-Margaretta found Madame Chatel painting as usual. But that scene was different from the still life Louisa-Margaretta had seen not half an hour before. Mademoiselle Chatel was with her. The subject, apparently, was some autumnal blooms and hothouse fruit that Mademoiselle Chatel was carefully arranging.

Louisa-Margaretta was angry to see them there, behaving as if nothing had happened. To think that all that time, they were responsible for the Duke's death, yet they had stood by while her family suffered! She would enjoy telling them how she and Judith had figured out the whole scheme, and she would force them to tell the magistrate.

"Madame," said Louisa-Margaretta. "Mademoiselle. I am very sorry to tell you this, but we have found you out."

Mademoiselle Chatel paled, but her mother did not look up from her painting.

"You English are so full of ideas! I could never understand what you mean."

"We mean that you killed the Duke," said Louisa-Margaretta.

Madame Chatel did not look up. "Nonsense."

"I am sure that it was, well, a matter of defending yourselves," said Judith. "Your honor."

"Honor has nothing to do with it," said Madame Chatel. "He was not an honourable man." At that, she looked up for the first time.

Louisa-Margaretta argued, "I'm not sure that justifies a killing."

"He must have attacked first," Judith said quietly. "And if a person were to defend herself from that attack, it is quite possible that it would happen in such a way as to injure him."

"I am sure he would never have attacked me," said Madame Chatel. "After all, I am old! Of course, if a so-called gentleman were to harm my daughter, I would defend her to my last breath."

Louisa-Margaretta looked at Judith, who shook her head. She was more than willing to hear the implication of the painter's words and believe it.

"We do not doubt you, madam," she said. She saw that Mademoiselle Chatel had covered her mouth with her hands. Judith walked over and touched the shoulder of the young woman, who began to weep.

"And you took the painting?" asked Louisa-Margaretta.

"No," said Judith. "The Duchess has been stealing them."

Both the Chatel ladies gasped. Louisa-Margaretta could see that they welcomed the distraction from their own roundabout confession. Madame Chatel did not appear nervous, but she had likely been wondering when another person would figure it out.

Judith, having worked out the matter of the thefts, seemed rather forlorn to Louisa-Margaretta.

"She is the only person who could have done it," said Judith. "She has been nearby during all of the sessions, and she was never suspected. And she had to live with such a man."

Louisa-Margaretta shook her head. All of the other ladies were speaking of the Duke as if he were the worst man they had ever met. She was not certain she could agree, but it was clever of Judith to have worked out who was behind the thefts.

"And Mr Galpin?" asked Louisa-Margaretta.

"He was a man who could not live with himself," said Madame Chatel. "I told him that he ought to tell your Mr Fletcher what his friend really was and that he ought to be ashamed of allowing the Duke to cover up such behavior for all the time they were together. He did not like this at all. He is afraid of a scandal himself, a coward until the last."

Louisa-Margaretta's temper flared. "So you know where he is?"

Madame Chatel waved one of her dainty hands. Though they were beautiful, Louisa-Margaretta knew that they worked just as hard as any labourer's. Madame Chatel had not allowed herself to rest since they came, even after the murder.

"I do not know where he is," said Madame Chatel. "But he will not be far. I'm sure he is hoping that the murderer can be caught and he can slink out of town after."

Louisa-Margaretta could not help sighing. "Oh, would to God that we could all leave this place! Madame Chatel, are you going back to London?"

The possibility of Mr Fortescue presented itself to her mind. She forced it aside just as quickly. Surely, there would be some alternative to marrying such a despicable man. If he took her, in her condition, she knew that it would give him yet one more excuse for tormenting her. She could not foresee raising a child with that sort of monster for a father.

"London?" Madame Chatel shook her head. "We shall pass through. But you will forgive me. Our horrid time here has taught us one thing. I must go with a daughter to a place where the way of life we lost in France is still respected. We two are bound for St Petersburg."

"Would you take me?" asked Louisa-Margaretta.

Mademoiselle Chatel, who had turned away, put down her handkerchief. "You would join us? Oh, Mama, how wonderful!"

Louisa-Margaretta looked pointedly at Madame Chatel. "I will need to be somewhere very quiet, where I am not known, in the summer. Or perhaps the spring."

She looked down. She knew exactly what she was saying and that it was a rather despicable lie. The implication was that the Duke had forced himself upon her and that a child would result. Judith gasped in horror, rushing over to her friend.

Louisa-Margaretta resolved to tell Judith the truth as soon as she could. But she could not fully trust Madame or Mademoiselle Chatel. If they knew who the natural father of her child was, they might tell someone. If they believed it to be the Duke, they would stay silent. Certainly, they would not wish to draw attention to their part in his murder.

Perhaps all of the sinners could do penance in Russia.

"Judith," said Louisa-Margaretta, "would you go? You know that I would not ask you. Only, I cannot ask Mama. She cannot know."

She saw how the words affected her friend. Judith, who had once mistakenly assumed that Louisa-Margaretta was carrying a child, had not suspected her recent troubles. Judith's face was suffused with sympathy and concern.

"Louisa-Margaretta," she said, and she embraced her friend. "But perhaps a hasty marriage?"

"Is not possible," said Louisa-Margaretta. "At least, not here. And if I am to find a husband and a position, I must do it quickly."

She could see Judith considering the matter. Her friend was not going to make such a decision in a rush, and she would be loath to leave her family. Then there was the whole matter of Cousin Morgan. Louisa-Margaretta would have advised her friend to give up on that match long ago, but she had seen just how strong the attachment was on both sides. Perhaps he could be persuaded to come with them. So far away, there could be no one who would object to the two of them marrying.

Madame Chatel was still hesitant. "It is a long journey. And though we have friends in that city, we shall not be living anywhere like this home."

"We do not mind," said Louisa-Margaretta. In fact, she did prefer surroundings that were at least as comfortable as the home her family kept in London. But thanks to her friendship with Judith, she had learned that she could tolerate much less, provided she was still permitted to ride regularly. She was more determined to guard her secret than she was to keep her beautiful domestic arrangements.

"Please," said Mademoiselle Chatel, and something passed between mother and daughter.

"Very well," said Madame Chatel. "But you all seem to have forgotten that my daughter and I have not yet been granted permission to leave."

Louisa-Margaretta choked back a scream of exasperation. All of the troubles she and Judith had been trying to wade through had seemed difficult enough, but that new difficulty made them feel impossible.

Judith was just as disturbed. She gave Louisa-Margaretta a long look. "How shall we ever deal with Mr Fletcher?"

Madame Chatel was thinking. "Your Mr Fletcher, is he fair, you think?"

Louisa-Margaretta shook her head, but Judith nodded. "Yes. I believe so."

Madame Chatel smiled. "Well, then, it is simple. I shall go to him and say that my daughter and I will not wait here at his pleasure. We are leaving, and if he chooses to lock us up or have us pursued, he may. An exiled painter and a young mademoiselle? He will look like a brute for doing it. I shall say that Mr Galpin has already left, so we should not be forced to stay when he is gone."

"You would blame it on an innocent?" Judith's eyes went wide.

"I will not say he is guilty," said Madame Chatel. "Only that, since he is gone, it would be silly to have all the rest of us stay."

"The only trouble is this," said Louisa-Margaretta. "Mr Fletcher is still going to believe that a man committed this act. And even if he trusts my father, he suspects my cousin. What are we to do about Cousin Morgan? If everyone else is gone, the blame will only fall on his shoulders."

Judith cleared her throat, looking down. "I have a notion of what might be done on that score."

48

———

Judith spent a moment thinking about how strange it was that her family was all gathered. They looked like a picture, she thought, her father and Miriam on one side of the room, her three brothers on the other.

She wanted to spend more than a moment treasuring the sight, as she knew she might soon be a stranger to all of them. But it was past time to tell them, and she felt only a fluttering of unease as she did. Her life could end at any moment—that was in the hands of God—and she did not want to go to her grave having denied Morgan.

"I have an announcement to make," she said. "I am engaged."

Miriam looked curious, and her brothers all looked at their father for a response. When they saw that he was smiling warmly, Aaron burst out, "Will you have to move again, then?"

He looked a little ashamed of his question. Judith's father came and sat next to her. "Thank you for telling us, dear," he said. "I am glad you have considered Mr Barnwell's offer. This is a blessing indeed."

Miriam was the only one in the room who frowned. Judith's brothers were already murmuring amongst themselves, ready for the rooms upstairs to be divided differently. If Miriam were to take Judith's, that would leave one room quite free!

"No, Papa," said Judith, colouring. Already, she was in such a muddle! "I have not accepted Mr Barnwell. It is Mr Morgan Ramsbury of whom I speak. He proposed, and I accepted, though I hope I can accept with your blessing all the same."

Her father looked astonished, Miriam elated.

"Oh, Judith!" She went to embrace her sister, but something in their father's eyes must have stopped her.

"This is most unexpected," said the rector. "Mr Barnwell had been telling me that he felt he could persuade you."

Judith shook her head firmly. "I do not know what he said, Papa, but I am sure I said nothing of the sort to him. If he is mistaken in his understanding, I am very sorry for it."

"Mr Barnwell is to leave, then?" asked Aaron, crossly.

"No," said Miriam, her voice sharp. "Nobody is leaving. Come, all of you. March! We ought to leave Judith with Papa. Your general will be very cross if you do not listen to orders."

She got her brothers into some sort of line and shepherded them all out of the room, with no more than one smile at Judith.

"Papa," said Judith. "I am sorry to distress you. I can assure you I did not give Mr Barnwell a false impression. He must have come up with that on his own."

"I am sure he is capable of leaping to judgement," said Papa.

"That is a subject upon which I continually attempt to instruct him. No, Judith, my concern is the church. Mr Ramsbury is a Quaker, is he not? So you cannot be married in the church."

"That is correct," said Judith.

"Where would you marry, then?"

"I am afraid I had not thought so far as that, Papa." Judith stared at her knees. She felt as if she were about to be admonished after lessons. Papa's gentle manner had always been terrifying. Her mother's brusque words, though harsher, were not quite so hard to bear. She wanted Mama to be there. Surely, her mother would have understood!

"Can you give us your blessing, Papa?" asked Judith. "I know I should not have kept it from you, only, I did not know how to tell all of you. I wondered whether I should still have a home here."

"I would never turn you out, Judith," he said slowly, and she could have wept with relief.

"But you cannot ask my blessing, not yet. I must be allowed time to contemplate this and to learn more of what our faith requires. I may confess, it never occurred to me that any of my children would wish to marry outside the church, you least of all."

Judith nodded, her throat feeling as if it were on fire. "How long, Papa?"

He shook his head, and she saw that he was also near tears. "I could not say, child."

49

"Thank you for telling Mr Fletcher my reason for visiting," said Morgan. "He was almost cordial when we parted."

"I should have spoken earlier," said Judith. "Forgive me?" She received only an embrace in response.

"I cannot see why thou must go with my cousin," Morgan said. "She has made her bed, has she not?"

Judith, enjoying the sensation of being clasped in her beloved's arms, his lips dangerously near her neck, did not answer right away.

"It is not only a question of Louisa-Margaretta's life. There is to be a child, who will also be your cousin and an innocent. Besides, as to her error, we are all sinners," she said firmly, and she felt quite justified in saying it to Morgan. After all, he and Judith had deliberately misled everyone about their respective whereabouts in order to steal a private walk in the hills together before the coaches left.

He chuckled. His breath was warm in her hair. "That is true enough."

She turned to face him, staying in his arms as they spoke

of an uncertain future. "Besides, I would not see thee even if I stayed," she said. "Vienna is very far."

"Dost thou disagree with me?" He looked down at her face in order to read her expression.

"No." She hesitated. "That is, I agree that it is important that our diplomats protect the greatest gains of the revolution. Only, I wish that my own love were not going, not when it is dangerous and perhaps even futile. I am allowed to wish such a thing, am I not?"

That made him smile. "Yes. Yes, of course."

They had no need for more words, not until Judith reminded him that they had better be going.

"Before someone comes to search for us," she said, trying to convince both him and herself.

When they went down from the hill, hand in hand, she saw Louisa-Margaretta waiting.

"Are you ready, Judith?" she asked. "We ought to be starting."

Judith clasped Morgan's hand tightly then released it. They would have another goodbye in front of the Wycliff Castle servants and their families, but that farewell would be calm and respectable.

"I am not ready," she said. "But we must start all the same."

TWO SPINSTERS AND A MADMAN

ALSO BY EVE TARRINGTON

Two Spinsters and a Corpse

Two Spinsters and a Duel

Two Spinsters and a Madman

Two Spinsters and an Assassin

ABOUT THE AUTHOR

Eve Tarrington is a Jane Austen fanatic. She has written dozens of books, but this is her first historical mystery set in the Regency era. She is thankful to her readers, her family, and her friends.

Would you like to know when Eve Tarrington is putting out a new novel? You're in luck! Join the mailing list at tena ciousteacuppress.com/eveTnews. You'll get an email when a new book is coming out.

In addition, you'll get a special copy of *Two Ladies and a Manhunt*, a subscriber bonus that follows young Judith and Louisa-Margaretta as they separately search for a young lady. When Louisa-Margaretta's friend disappears from one of the most exclusive London ballrooms shortly after coming out, suspicions and false accusations fly. For very different reasons, Judith and Louisa-Margaretta, still strangers, are intent on finding her killer.